"I
me

The Nina
kep ed
her

The
faces.

Bret's expression faded from that of a proud parent to deep concern. She should explain, but her heart was being shredded.

"Girls, why don't you go back to my office? I'll be there in a minute."

The minute the girls were gone, she wrapped her arms around her waist.

"Are you all right? I never considered that you might not like children."

"I like children."

"Really? You went pale as a ghost."

"I was surprised, that's all." Tears filled her eyes.

"Nina. What's going on?"

"Nothing. I'm fine." The sob escaped her throat.

Bret steered her toward the sofa and sat beside her. "I'm not leaving until you tell me what's wrong."

She stared into Bret's eyes. He was safe. Trustworthy. Why was it so hard to say the words?

"I had a daughter. She died. Five years ago today."

**Lorraine Beatty** was raised in Columbus, Ohio, but now calls Mississippi home. She and her husband, Joe, have two sons and five grandchildren. Lorraine started writing in junior high and is a member of RWA and ACFW, and is a charter member and past president of Magnolia State Romance Writers. In her spare time she likes to work in her garden, travel and spend time with her family.

## Books by Lorraine Beatty

### Love Inspired

#### *Mississippi Hearts*

*Her Fresh Start Family*

#### *Home to Dover*

*Protecting the Widow's Heart*
*His Small-Town Family*
*Bachelor to the Rescue*
*Her Christmas Hero*
*The Nanny's Secret Child*
*A Mom for Christmas*
*The Lawman's Secret Son*
*Her Handyman Hero*

# Her Fresh Start Family

## Lorraine Beatty

HARLEQUIN® LOVE INSPIRED®

Recycling programs
for this product may
not exist in your area.

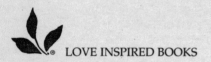

LOVE INSPIRED BOOKS

ISBN-13: 978-1-335-42814-1

Her Fresh Start Family

Copyright © 2018 by Lorraine Beatty

www.Harlequin.com

**Printed in U.S.A.**

This is the day which the Lord hath made;
we will rejoice and be glad in it.
—*Psalms* 118:24

To my mother-in-law, Mary Beatty.
You are one of my greatest blessings.

# Chapter One

A warm morning breeze blew a strand of Nina Johnson's hair across her eyes. She pulled it away, her gaze riveted on the building in front of her. The two-story brick structure had an abundance of windows and a recessed entry that allowed for shade to cover the entrance. It looked fairly new. Had the cabdriver made a mistake and left her at the wrong place? She pulled her phone from her purse and brought up the address. It read 557 E. Warren Avenue. Her spirits sagged. She should never have agreed to come here. But then, where else would she have gone? Kathryn Harvey was her closest friend. She'd been there for her since college, through the marriage and the dark days afterward. When she'd asked her to come down to Hastings, Mississippi, and take over her psychology practice while she and her husband took advantage of a job in Spain for the next few months, she hadn't been able to refuse. Her position as a corporate psychologist at Duncan and Stone had been eliminated. The call from her friend had been a blessing. Until now.

"Can I help you?"

Nina started at the sound of the deep voice close beside her. She stepped away, glancing at the man. Her gaze lifted until she found his startling green eyes lit with a smile. "No, I'm fine. Thank you."

"You looked lost."

The man was inquisitive for a stranger. She moved away a little more. "No, just surprised. The building is so small." He frowned, and she realized she might have insulted him, so she hastened to explain. "My previous job was in a high-rise. Twentieth floor."

"Ah. Not too many high-rises around here. But I assure you, this building is big enough to house seven thriving businesses. I should know. One of them is mine." He held out his hand. "I'm Bret Sinclair."

With her hands full of her purse, briefcase and a satchel filled with books she thought she might need, she could only stare back at him. She wasn't used to strange men boldly intro-ducing themselves—and shaking hands was even pushier. He didn't seem to be the least bit put off by her nonresponse.

"Sorry. Let me help you."

He took the briefcase from her grasp before she could react.

She had little choice but to introduce herself. "I'm Nina Johnson." His large hand swallowed hers, wrapping around it with a solid strength that gave her an uneasy feeling, yet she was strangely reluctant to pull her hand away. The stress of the trip down here to Hastings must be getting to her.

A big smile spread across the man's olive-toned skin, revealing a row of straight white teeth and an angled jawline that was very attractive.

"Kitty's friend. She told us you'd be filling in for her. Nice to meet you. Let me show you to your office."

She retrieved her briefcase from the man. "Kitty?"

"Yeah, we all call her that. Kathryn didn't suit her personality."

Nina mulled that over as she entered through the door the man held open. When had her friend taken the nickname? But then, she'd allowed their friendship to fade over the last few years, and she'd admittedly been surprised when Kathryn had asked her to take over her practice for a few months. Nina had closed her private practice years ago and gone into corporate psychology. She'd loved it. The job allowed her to help others, while not getting personally involved with patients or becoming emotionally attached. Things she'd vowed to avoid.

The man, Mr. Sinclair, walked briskly toward the end of the hall, and she had a hard time keeping up with him in her four-inch heels. The floor was slippery, too. He was chattering about something, but all she could think of was getting to Kathryn's office and closing the door.

"Anita owns the Tranquility Spa. She does it all from hair and nails to facials and those crazy body wraps. You'll have a full-service business when you want to get dolled up."

Was he suggesting she needed a makeover? She gritted her teeth and tried to keep up. Was he deliberately trying to be offensive? She'd been to a spa once and found it anything but relaxing. She glanced at her host and found him still smiling. His unusual green eyes held a twinkle as he looked down at her. She averted her gaze. Something about the man made her uncomfortable. No doubt his overly solicitous attitude was the source. This Sinclair guy was far too friendly for her liking.

He pushed the button beside the elevator door and waited while she entered first.

"Your office is on the second floor."

He continued his diatribe, throwing out names and businesses as if she were interested in the other occupants of the building. Stealing a glance at her host, she sorted through her people cubbies to find a good slot in which to file him away. On the surface, he seemed nice enough, but he was trying too hard to be helpful, and that usually meant he'd attempt to insert himself into her life. That was the last thing she wanted. When the elevator opened, she stepped out briskly, hoping he'd point out the right door and then go away.

"I'm right across the hall."

Nina pulled her attention back to the man. "Excuse me?"

His grin deepened, exposing a dimple on the right side of his mouth that she'd failed to notice before. It was a nice dimple.

"At the moment, the only businesses on the second floor are yours, mine and David Ellis's, the photographer. The last office is empty, and back there is the break room." He pointed to the door to his right. "That's my company. Phase II. We help veterans with training and job placement, and whatever else they might need when they're ready to reenter the workforce."

Nina's heart lurched. "Soldiers?"

"As a matter of fact, we're organizing our annual Military Appreciation Day event, and we're always looking for volunteers. We'd welcome your help."

"I don't think so."

"You have something against soldiers?"

He asked the question with a teasing tone in his voice. She cast a stern look in his direction. "Only when they fail to do their job and people die." Clearly caught off guard, he frowned and rubbed his forehead. The smile left his face, calling attention to the sharp angle of his jaw and his high cheekbones. The clear green eyes had darkened to a dull forest color.

"Aren't there dozens of organizations already helping veterans?"

"There are, but most of them are located two hours away, up in the state capital, and the waiting lists for those organizations are long. The vets need services here, where they live."

His sincerity and passion caught her off guard, leaving her without a comeback. Thankfully she spotted the plaque on the wall beside the door on the left. Kathryn Harvey Psychologist. Nina fished out the key Kathryn had sent, but before she could use it, Bret opened the door and smiled down at her. "You have a key to this office?"

"To all of them. I own the building. Which makes me the landlord. But don't worry. I don't enter anyone's business unless it's an emergency."

"Is that what this is?"

He chuckled as if she'd said something funny. The rich, throaty sound sent a quick ping along her nerves.

"No. I'm the welcome committee. I promised Kitty I'd help you settle in. When you get a free moment, I'll introduce you to the others. We all try and look out for one another."

Nina shrank in on herself. She needed to escape his overly helpful greeting right now. "That's very kind, but I don't need any help, and I doubt I'll have much time for socializing."

She squared her shoulders and marched into the small reception area, striving for an air of supreme confidence that would deter any further help. Instead she caught her heel in the overly plush carpet and tripped, quickly regaining her balance. Pulse racing, she placed her belongings on the desk and turned to face him. "Thank you for your help. I can take it from here."

His hand was outstretched as if he'd intended to steady her, which he could easily have done, given his broad, well-developed shoulders and forearms. The black polo shirt with the Phase II logo on the breast pocket, and the faded jeans he wore, made it obvious that he enjoyed working out.

"Those shoes are dangerous. You could hurt yourself."

Incredible. First a makeover, and now her shoes? Criticism was the last thing she needed at this moment. Her nerves were frayed. She attempted a firm expression. "Mr. Sinclair, I have a lot of studying to do before I see my first patient. I'm sure you'll understand if I don't have time to visit."

He stared at her for a moment, his green eyes probing, making her regret her retort. She reminded herself she was here to fill in for Kathryn and reacquaint herself with working one-on-one with private patients. Not to get chummy with the natives.

"Okay then. If you need anything or have any questions, I'm right over there." He gestured to the office across the hall.

She grasped the doorknob and met his gaze. The puzzlement in his eyes turned the green to a dull moss color. Very curious.

"Sure thing." He started out the door, but stopped it from closing with his hand. She couldn't help but notice it was a very attractive hand with long blunt fingers at the end of a muscled forearm. She pressed her lips together. She was more stressed than she thought. The man was smiling again.

"Dottie will be here shortly. She knows everything there is to know about Kitty's patients. Except the private stuff, of course."

Nina managed a stiff smile and pushed on the door again. Finally the man left, and she leaned against the door, taking a few deep breaths to calm her nerves. Silence. Alone. Now she could think and process.

As she turned around, she caught sight of him entering his office, and he lifted his hand in a wave. To her dismay, she could see a great deal of his offices through the row of glass windows. Great. The man was a serious threat to her powers of concentration. Reaching up, she closed the blinds, restoring her sense of security.

Her gaze took in the tastefully decorated area, which was furnished with a reception desk, a half dozen comfortable chairs and a coffee table piled with magazines. To the right of the desk was a door, which she guessed led to her friend's office. Given Kathryn's bubbly personality, she'd expected frilly, feminine decor, but the room had been decorated in calm and soothing tones of green and egg-shell—perfect for helping patients relax.

An assortment of upholstered furniture in a muted fabric filled the space. Kathryn's desk sat at one end of the room, in front of a wall of shelves holding countless books. A tall file cabinet stood nearby.

A quick check of the other doors revealed a small bathroom and a tiny lunch room. The arrangement suited her. She could come to work and never have to leave the office until the end of the day. Perfect.

A folder with her name on it rested in the middle of the desk. She sat down and opened the cover and read the letter inside. Kathryn started off by apologizing for not being there to help her get settled. The job overseas had opened up sooner than expected, and they'd had to leave. She explained that she had transferred the most critical patients to other qualified professionals. The rest, she had assured her, were mainly in need of weekly talk time and reassurance.

In addition, Kathryn had given her a schedule, a patient list and all the information she'd need to do her job. She'd also encouraged her to take on new patients if she wanted. But the last item on the list sent her heart into her throat. Once a week, she would be counseling a group of widows who were working through the changes in their lives as they started to move beyond the initial grieving period and transition into a normal life.

Nina touched her trembling fingertips to her lips. No. She couldn't possibly counsel widows. She was a widow, and she'd avoided dealing with her loss for the last several years. It was why she'd closed her private practice and gone to work for Duncan. Her job consisted of interviewing potential employees and assigning them to the best positions. It was all superficial and didn't require her to become emotionally involved.

But it was the P.S. at the end of Kitty's letter that sent a cold rush along her veins. "I left my car parked behind the building, and the keys are in the drawer. I know you probably won't use them, but just in case you do." Nina's throat closed up. Why would Kathryn think for one moment she would use those keys? The thought of getting behind the wheel of a car turned her blood to ice. At least, that was one area she didn't have to worry about. But how was she going to deal with a group of widows needing guidance and direction when she had nothing whatsoever to offer them?

\* \* \*

Bret retreated into his office, taking a seat in his worn leather chair and swinging it around to stare out the window. He could see the historic Saint John's church steeple from here, and the sight normally grounded him. But at the moment, his mind was churning with confusion. Nina Johnson wasn't what he'd expected. Kitty had described her friend as sweet and compassionate, a born nurturer with a heart for others. Kitty had mentioned that Nina had experienced great sadness in her life, but she hadn't elaborated. Kitty would never reveal personal information about her patients or her friends.

But the woman in her office now was cool, distant and might as well have worn a sign warning everyone to stay away. Yet Bret had seen her true emotions reflected in her blue eyes. They'd been filled with anxiety as she'd stared at the building, but then she'd quickly masked that anxiety behind a cool demeanor. Later he'd seen regret and anger dart through her eyes when he'd explained about his company. Her comment about soldiers didn't sit well.

Kitty's depiction of Nina Johnson didn't match the exterior of the woman either. Her five-foot-five frame was slender with rigid posture, and the gray suit and white blouse she wore did little to accentuate her bright blue eyes or her rich chestnut hair, which she wore clipped back behind her ears.

He suspected her prim image was a shield for her deep vulnerability. He'd seen similar behavior in the veterans he worked with. Many of them chose to hide their feelings and fears instead of dealing with them. He and Kitty used to tease each other that he provided the external tools with his job placement and training programs, and she provided the internal tools by showing soldiers how to confront their fears and overcome them. She was also a strong supporter of his goal to provide help and assistance for the soldiers.

He spun in his chair and opened his computer. Nina's comment about soldiers left him uneasy. If Nina had issues with veterans, she might have a hard time fitting in with the others. Everyone in the building helped with the Military Appreciation Day event, and many of Kitty's patients were veterans. Would Kitty's replacement be able to connect with them in the same way Kitty had? He hoped so. He knew how hard Kitty worked to help those in her care. He hoped Nina wouldn't inadvertently set them back.

Rapid tapping on his door broke into his

thoughts. His friend and business partner, Alan McKay, strolled in and perched himself on the edge of the desk.

"So, I hear the new lady is here. Is she pretty? Single? Looking for a handsome guy to show her around?"

If Alan was half as attractive as he thought he was, he'd be dangerous. "She's attractive in a business kind of way." He wasn't about to give his friend any ammunition by telling him about the odd attraction he'd felt when he saw her standing in front of the building. She'd looked like a little girl who'd lost her way. When he'd looked into her eyes, he'd realized she was a woman fighting to get through the next moment without losing it. The same way he was. The realization rocked him. Was that how people saw him, keeping a tight rein on his emotions, afraid to set his heart free? He put on a good show. He was friendly and jovial, but inside, he was battling to hold it together. So what was Nina Johnson's story?

"Meaning what?"

"She's reserved and a bit closed off." He rested his arms on the desk. "She reminds me of Olivia."

"Your eight-year-old? How so?"

"She's smart and funny most of the time, but away from the family, she is painfully shy.

It takes time for her to assess the situation before she'll step into the action. Maybe all Miss Nina needs is a little time to adjust to her environment."

Alan crossed his arm over his chest. "Or maybe she's like your five-year-old. Outgoing and ready for fun, but she just didn't warm to you." He stood. "I'm going to go over there and say welcome."

Bret's protective instincts kicked in. "Alan, I don't think that's such a good idea. It's her first day, and she seemed really nervous. Give her some time to settle in before you go throwing your charm around."

"Yeah, I suppose you're right. But be sure and invite her to the monthly birthday party tomorrow. Then we can all meet her and welcome her into the family."

"I will, but I don't think she's the sociable type. She might not want to be buddies with the other business owners." The idea saddened him. Kitty had spent much of her free time visiting the other tenants. He had a feeling Nina was more comfortable by herself. Getting her to join the fun would be a tough job. A surge of determination grew in his mind. He wanted her to be part of the group, and he wouldn't stop until he knew her story and had her firmly integrated into their family. He'd been the outsider once, and the people here had given him back the sense of belonging he'd lost when his wife walked out.

Alan leaned forward with a grin. "So, do I detect some interest on your part? Did the lady capture your attention?"

Bret shook his head and turned his focus to the computer screen. "I have no desire to get involved with anyone." But he couldn't deny that something about the new therapist intrigued him. Those big blue eyes in the pretty oval face had lodged in his mind, and the sweet, flowery scent she wore still lingered in his nostrils, though it was at odds with her closed-off attitude.

"I promised Kitty I'd look after her and help her get adjusted. That's all." Strictly for the sake of her patients, of course, and Kitty's reputation. He had a sudden desire to see the lady with her hair down. Literally and figuratively.

"Dude, you need to get your nose out of this job and start noticing women again."

"You're the ladies' man around here. Not me. My two little girls are the only women I need in my life."

"Bret, old buddy, I've known you since we were on the football team in high school, and I know you're a family man to the core. You don't do well single. You're happiest when you're part of a couple. Married."

Bret punched the enter key on his laptop with more force than necessary. His friend was right, but he wasn't going to risk his heart again, or those of his little girls. "I tried that, remember? I failed miserably. Dad and I are doing okay raising the girls."

Alan exhaled an exasperated breath. This wasn't the first time they'd had this conversation.

"Don't you think you deserve another chance? Maybe, with the right woman, things would be different."

"And maybe they wouldn't. It wasn't the woman. It was me."

"Not true. One of these days, you're going to have to let go of those black bags of guilt you're still carrying around over that thing in Afghanistan and your wife and allow yourself to be happy again. Lay it at the cross, man. Lay it at the cross. I gotta go. I got to see a man about a donation."

Alan's uninhibited personality was a huge asset to Phase II. He had a way of loosening purse strings and opening wallets and getting donations that kept the business afloat. "Hope it's a big one." While they charged for many of their services, the donations allowed them to keep the cost of classes and training manageable for the veterans who were on tight budgets. Their main goal was to acquire a government contract that would cover expenses on a permanent basis. So far, no luck in that department, but he felt sure Alan's bulldog determination and his attention to detail would get them a contract this time around. "How's it going on that contract application?"

"Good, but I want to make sure I cross every *T* and dot every *I* before I submit it. How about you? How's the Military Appreciation Day event coming along?"

"I have a chamber-of-commerce meeting tomorrow. I'm not hopeful of them planning anything different this year."

"You mean, other than throwing up a few tents and handing out flyers? That didn't generate much interest last year. We need publicity. Radio, TV, word of mouth. And we need to make it a fun family day."

"I agree. Now we just need to convince the members to let go of some money to make it happen."

Bret was relieved when Alan left the office. His friend meant well, but he didn't fully understand the heavy burden he carried deep inside. He'd tried to reconcile his failures in his mission and his marriage, but nothing had eased his guilt in the last three years, and he doubted anything ever would. All he could do was try to make up for it with his company, help as many veterans as possible and take care of his girls.

No time to think of that now. He had a class to prepare for. Six vets had signed up for computer classes this afternoon, and he hadn't even prepared the classroom.

He stood up and walked through the office, his gaze darting to the front door and the office across the hall. How was Nina getting along? Hopefully her secretary, Dottie, would ease her transition. Something told him that Nina had more than just nerves over a new position to contend with. He had a gut feeling that her issues ran as deep as his.

Nina leaned back in her chair—Kathryn's chair—and closed her eyes. Most of her earlier anxiety had faded in the soothing privacy of the office. She discovered a pod coffee maker and made herself a cup. The flavored brew settled her nerves. All she needed now was a cup of confidence to go along with it. Her landlord had more than his share of confidence. Normally, that would be an indication that a person was well-adjusted, but he'd overdone the welcome, as far as she was concerned. It probably had something to do with his good looks. He knew he was handsome and behaved accordingly.

She had to admit he had a nice smile and warm, friendly eyes. His close-cropped dark brown hair was long enough to hint at a tendency to wave and gave him a boyish quality.

What was she doing? She set her cup down and shoved her thoughts of Bret Sinclair aside. She had no time to think about anything but her reason for being here. Her goal was to come to the office, meet with her patients, help them in any way she could and keep them on track until Kathryn and her family returned home. When she wasn't at the office, she would keep to herself. Alone. Quiet. Avoiding the past.

Carrying her cup out to the reception area, she peeked out into the corridor separating the various offices. Sinclair had said there were seven businesses in the building, and he'd seemed eager to introduce her to the owners. She'd have to make sure she was too busy to get involved.

Movement across the hall caught her attention. The offices of Phase II took up the whole west side of the second level. Wide windows on either side of the main entry afforded a clear view of the reception area. A young woman sat at the desk, while people moved back and forth, some in military uniforms. Would they be coming and going all day? The thought twisted a small spot under her breastbone. She wouldn't think about that.

Bret suddenly came into sight and spoke with the woman at the desk. Nina froze. Then, as if sensing her staring, he rotated and looked directly at her. He smiled, sending a slow, warm wave of awareness through her body. She told herself it was embarrassment at being caught snooping, but she knew it was more than that. The warmth in his green eyes could be felt through the glass. She gave a slight nod and hurriedly turned away.

She didn't want to give the man any ideas. As she started back to her desk, she heard the office door swish open. Was he coming to talk to her again? Quickly, she formed a plausible excuse to turn him away, but when she looked over her shoulder, it wasn't Bret, but a middle-aged woman with a bright smile, perfectly coiffed light brown hair and glasses on a chain hanging around her neck.

"Hello, there. I'm Dottie Patterson. Welcome to Hastings. I'm so excited to have you here. Kitty thinks the world of you."

The woman's sincere greeting and easy manner instantly calmed Nina's nerves. "Glad to meet you, Dottie. Kathryn told me you had the answers for all my questions."

"Ha. Sounds like her." Dottie piled her purse and several bags onto the desktop. "No. I only have a few answers, but I do know where all the bodies are buried." She waved her hand. "Just joking. I will help you with everything I can. I'm familiar with her schedule and most of her patients, though of course, not their issues. But I know enough to detect when they really need to see her, or when they just need a kind word."

The idea of having a filter between herself and her patients was reassuring. "You must have worked for her a long time?"

"Since her boys were babies. Course, I only work three days a week now. Monday through Wednesdays, till noon. Hubby is retired, and I want to spend as much time together as we can."

"Kathryn doesn't have a full load of patients?"

"She used to, but a year ago, she decided she needed to spend more time with her family, so she started pulling back. Now she sees patients early in the week. Thursday is for emergencies or new patients, and Friday, she plays hooky."

"Sounds like a nice job, but I prefer to be busy. I don't do well with time on my hands."

"I hope you don't go stir crazy here, then. We aren't very busy. Kitty has transferred her most serious patients to other qualified doctors. You'll be working mainly with the run-of-the-mill neurosis and phobias."

"I wasn't aware there were any of those."

Dottie chuckled. "Sorry. You know what I mean. At any rate, I'll help you all I can, and of course, you're welcome to take on any new patients if you like. In your spare time, you can discover Hastings. It's a very historic town. We have dozens of antebellum homes, a cemetery dating back to the settling of the area and several notable museums."

Dottie turned on the computer, and then she planted her hands on her hips. "Did you read the letter Kitty left?"

"Yes. It all seemed pretty simple."

"Good. The only really important item is the Widow's Walk Club. That's every Tuesday night at 6:30."

Nina's palms began to sweat at the thought of the one thing she wished she could avoid. "I'm afraid I haven't had much experience in group therapy. I'm more comfortable with one-on-one sessions."

"Oh, don't worry about that. These ladies

have been in the group for years now. They've been through it all together. All you have to do is listen and make sure they're being honest with themselves."

"Any chance we could suspend the group until Kathryn returns?"

Dottie raised her head and frowned. "Goodness, no. Those women depend on that weekly meeting. For a couple of them, it's all that's keeping them grounded."

Dottie must have seen her alarm. She came and gave her shoulders a warm squeeze. "Don't worry. The women are all sweet as pie, and they'll bring you up to speed. They are looking forward to meeting you. Now, let's get you settled in."

The next few hours were spent going over everything with Dottie. They sorted the patient files to coordinate with each appointment so Nina could read them before they met. The only bump in the road was the patient scheduled for this afternoon. Dottie had tried to reschedule but was unable. Nina wasn't prepared to counsel someone this soon, but she had no choice. She'd come here to shake herself out of her apathetic state, so jumping in with both feet might be a good thing.

Thankfully the patient called and canceled at the last minute. All she wanted to do now was get to her hotel, take a long bath and study the files for tomorrow. She had five appointments during the day, and the Widow's Walk group in the evening. It was going to be a long day.

After placing a call for a cab, Nina gathered her belongings and headed downstairs. She stepped out the front door of the building and into the heat. It must be eighty-five degrees, much too hot for a wool suit. Maybe she'd shed the jacket tomorrow. Mid-April in Chicago was still cold, damp and sometimes snowy. Here in Southern Mississippi, the sun shone, and the flowers were blooming. It was a nice surprise, but she prayed there wouldn't be too many more. She liked things predictable, controlled. Her first day had been anything but.

Glancing at her watch, and then up the street, she willed the cab to arrive. She was tired, cranky and hot, and all she wanted to do was get to her hotel room and shut out the world and everyone in it.

Bret Sinclair's grin flashed through her mind. He was someone she definitely wanted to block out.

The only way she could survive these next few months was to keep to herself. She couldn't risk getting emotionally involved again, because risking another loss of someone she loved would kill her.

It almost had the first time.

# Chapter Two

Bret finished straightening his desk, closed his laptop and prepared to leave for the day. As he pushed his chair under his desk, he glanced out the window and caught sight of someone below standing on the front sidewalk. Nina. He peered closer. She had her hands full of her briefcase and satchel again, and that monster purse she carried. What was she doing standing in the hot sun?

She was still there when he exited the front door. He glanced around but didn't see a car or taxi anywhere.

"Are you waiting for someone?"

She jerked and emitted a soft gasp. "You shouldn't sneak up on people."

"Didn't mean to. So, how did the first day go?"

"Fine, but I've got a lot of homework to do

before I see my first patient tomorrow." Nina checked her watch again.

"I noticed you'd been standing here awhile. I got concerned. What are you doing?"

"Waiting for my cab."

Bret tugged on his earlobe. "Then you may have a long wait. Taxis here are not very reliable."

"The dispatcher said the cab would be here in five minutes."

"And how long ago was that?"

Nina hesitated a moment before responding. "Twenty minutes."

"No surprise there. You'll probably have to rent a car if you want to get around."

"That's not an option. I don't drive."

"At all?" His eyes widened, and a frown creased his forehead.

"No."

"Well, how did you manage to get around in Chicago?"

"Public transportation, cabs, the EL." She looked up and down the street. "I assumed I could hire a cab here. I didn't have any trouble this morning."

"You were fortunate. Don't expect that kind of service every time you call them. They're okay if you don't have to be someplace on time. There's only one taxi company in Hastings, and they're spread pretty thin. They do the best they can."

She shifted her case from one hand to the other. He could clearly see the fatigue etched in the pinched corners of her mouth and furrowed brow. In the heavy suit and jacket, she had to be melting in the heat.

"You can't stand out here forever. Why don't I drop you off. Where are you staying?"

She hesitated, glancing once more at her watch, clearly reluctant to accept his offer. The heat must have forced her to decide. "The Emerald Hotel, downtown Hastings."

It was the most expensive hotel in the city. Didn't she realize there were several other more reasonably priced places across town? He reached out and took the briefcase from her hand. "That's on my way home. My car's out back." He gestured toward the walk along the side of the building.

"All right. Thank you."

He opened the door of his dark SUV and tossed a pink jacket into the back seat so she could sit down in the front. Safely buckled in, he started the engine and upped the fan speed on the AC. He stifled a grin when she sighed and unbuttoned her jacket to allow the cool air to wash over her. Adjusting to the heat in the Deep South took a lot of folks by surprise. He drove in silence along the Campbell highway, getting caught by every traffic light. When he turned off onto Franklin Street, he couldn't stand the quiet ant longer. "Kitty said you'll be here for three months, while they're overseas."

"Yes."

"I guess moving to Mississippi from the Windy City is a bit of a culture shock."

"I have to admit, I wasn't prepared. Kathryn said this was a thriving city. I'd expected it to be much bigger."

"It's actually not that small. We have a university, a new mall, and several national companies have made Hastings their home base. But no, we can't compete with Chicago in size, but we're growing."

"I'm sorry. That sounded rude. I'm just tired."

"I understand. Mississippi gets a bad rap most of the time. Give us a chance."

He pulled up at the curb in front of the hotel, and she opened the door the moment he came to a stop. He wasn't sure whether to be offended or take her at her word that she was tired and eager to relax.

"Thank you. I appreciate it."

He smiled. "You're welcome. What time do you want me to pick you up tomorrow morning?"

Her blue eyes widened. "Oh, I couldn't impose. I'll call the cab company sooner."

"You might still be late to work. Easier if I come and get you. What time do you usually start your day?"

"Eight thirty."

"Perfect. I usually arrive then, too. See you tomorrow. About eight fifteen."

Bret watched Nina until she disappeared through the elegant front door of the old hotel. She really didn't like taking help from him, and he couldn't help but wonder why. Some of her aloof attitude might be explained by being a Yankee. But he had a feeling there was more behind her standoffish personality. Something more serious than a change in regions.

If she allowed him to be her chauffeur, he might be able to figure her out and help her adjust. He also had a feeling she needed a friend.

As he entered his 1940s-Craftsman house, a short while later, he inhaled the aroma of something delicious that made his stomach growl. He found his dad standing at the stove.

His father glanced over his shoulder and scowled.

"You're late."

Bret was in no mood to do battle with his

dad tonight. "A friend needed a ride home from work. It was on the way, so…"

"Where to? Timbuktu?"

"The Emerald, downtown."

His dad scowled deeper. "That's not on your way home."

"It was today. What's for supper?"

"Roast beef and noodles, and you almost missed it."

"Where are my girls?"

"In the playhouse. Call them in. It's time to eat."

Bret headed toward the back door. He was thankful every day that his father was helping him raise his little girls, but there were things he and his dad didn't see eye to eye on. Bret walked to the edge of the deck and stood straight as an arrow. "Hear ye. Hear ye. Are there any princesses on the premises?"

Squeals and giggles greeted him as two little brown-haired girls dashed from the pink-and-white playhouse toward him. At five and eight years old, they were growing up too fast for his liking. He knelt down just in time to grab them both in a big bear hug.

"We're so glad you're home." Olivia smiled and patted his shoulder.

"I love it when you come home, Daddy."

Five-year-old Georgiana buried her head in the crook of his neck.

"I love coming home to my girls. Gramps has supper ready. Go get cleaned up so we can eat. And use soap."

Bret's eyes grew moist as he watched his daughters go inside. He loved them more than he could bear, and he wanted so much for both of them. He would do anything for them. But his failure as a husband had caused Sylvia to walk out on the three of them, leaving his children without a mother to love and nurture them as they grew. He'd tried his best to make up for the vacancy in the girls' lives, but there was only so much a father could do.

He shook off the gloomy thoughts. He'd learned it didn't do any good and only made him feel worse. Instead, he focused on the girls' sweet faces and their happy smiles. It always lifted his spirits. After all, Livvy and Georgie were all that mattered to him.

The evening meal passed with the usual chatter from the girls, a spilled glass of milk and a round of the old "she started it, no she did" game.

Bret stacked the dishes beside the sink, as his father scraped them off and loaded them into the dishwasher.

"So, who was this friend you took home?"

"She's the therapist filling in for Kitty."

"Single?"

"I don't know."

"Well, find out. Is she old, young, homely, what?"

Bret fought to curb his irritation. His dad was convinced that, if his son would just try marriage again, it would all work out. He'd never liked Sylvia. Always claimed she wasn't honest, and wasn't as committed to the marriage as he was. Bret spent a lot of his marriage overseas, serving in the army, and he always thought his dad was being his usual critical self. When he came home, things seemed fine to him. Until his last tour of duty.

He'd royally screwed up his mission assignment. He'd allowed the soldier he was sworn to protect with his life die. He'd barely had time to adjust to that debacle, when Sylvia had walked out, leaving the girls with his dad.

With his enlistment almost up, he'd taken an early discharge and gone home. But it was too late to save his marriage. He'd sold his house, moved in with his dad and put all his assets into purchasing the building and starting Phase II. He devoted his life now to helping veterans and being the best dad possible for his girls.

"Dad, I'm not looking for any relationship.

When would I have the time?" With two massive failures in responsibility, he wasn't looking for a chance to mess up again.

"That's what I'm here for."

"You do enough as it is."

"I'd do more if it meant you were happy and settled again. With the right woman this time."

"There's no way to know if she's right or not." He'd loved Sylvia. He'd believed their marriage was good.

"I'll know. I picked your mother, didn't I? I'd find a good woman for you, too, if you'd cooperate."

His dad meant well, but he didn't understand the thin veneer of emotional scar tissue that could be easily opened, allowing the old pain and guilt to seep through his whole being. "Right now I need to get two little girls to cooperate and get to bed."

Bedtime was always hectic, but he wouldn't trade it for peace and quiet. The little smiles, the hugs, the giggles, even the arguments, made him feel alive and filled him with hope. He prayed every day that the Lord would take up any slack left by his ineptitude. He was trusting the Almighty completely.

Bret closed the door to the girls' room, pausing a moment to snag one last glance at the precious, beautiful treasures. Oh, how he longed to protect them from the bumps and bruises of life. He'd had a similar feeling when he'd first met Nina. He had the overpowering sense that she needed protecting, despite her independent facade.

She was a puzzle, and he wanted to put all her pieces together to find out who she really was. This was the first time in years that he'd been drawn to a woman. Better not let his dad know he was interested. Besides, Bret knew he'd picked poorly the first time, and he'd likely repeat that mistake. In fact, he was. The first woman he'd noticed in years and she wasn't the warm and motherly type, but cool, distant and aloof. He really knew how to pick them.

No. He'd keep his interest in Nina as simply that. Interest. Thankfully, she was only going to be here a short while, and then she'd return to Yankee Land and all would be well. So why was he looking forward to seeing her again in the morning?

He was an idiot.

Safe in her hotel room, Nina soaked in a hot tub until the water cooled. Then she slipped into lounge pants and an oversize shirt, before ordering room service. She settled down with the files she'd brought home, but concentrating was difficult. Coming here was the biggest mistake of her life. Today had made that perfectly clear. She didn't belong here. She'd had visions of slipping quietly into Kathryn's job, reacquainting herself with counseling private patients and passing the days until her friend returned.

She hadn't counted on a man who had made it his job to look after her, or a secretary who was cheerier than a songbird at first light. Neither was she prepared for the warm weather and the lack of transportation. She should have done her research and been more proactive before accepting Kathryn's offer.

Nina rested her head on the small sofa in her room, digging her fingertips into the hair at her temples. No. She had to stop being a hermit, hiding away from life. That was why she'd come here—to shake herself out of the dull, unfeeling life she'd had before. Losing her job had forced her to see what she'd become. A sad, lonely, closed-off human being. She didn't like that person, but she'd lived this way so long, she didn't know how else to be. The offer from Kathryn was the answer to her prayers.

Her gaze landed on the stack of files she'd brought home. She had people depending on her. Patients who needed her. There wasn't time to feel sorry for herself. She picked up the folder, opened it and got to work.

Nina awoke the next morning with a nervous jitter dancing in her stomach. She would see her first patients today. She'd read their files, understood their issues, but it had been a long time since she'd counseled a patient privately. She decided to take it slowly today and allow herself to get a feel for each person who came into her office.

She dressed quickly and gathered her belongings, wanting to be downstairs, in front of the hotel, when Bret arrived. She'd have to find another way to and from work soon. She couldn't ride back and forth with her landlord every day. Heat enveloped her from the moment she stepped outside. Beads of sweat formed on her forehead. Her silk blouse clung to her skin, and the thick wool jacket became itchy and uncomfortable. She hoped Bret was on time, or else she'd be a wilted mess by the time she got to the office.

The big black SUV appeared around the corner, and she quickly climbed inside, relieved to feel the cool interior chasing away the heat.

"Good morning. Did you have a good night?"

"Yes. I did."

Bret scanned her outfit with a puzzled frown. "Aren't you hot?"

She tugged at her jacket, aware of the blouse still plastered to her skin. Still, she wasn't about to admit that. "No. It's my first day seeing patients. I need to look professional."

He shrugged. "If you say so."

Prickles of irritation formed. Why did he feel he had the right to criticize her attire? "What's wrong with what I'm wearing?"

"Nothing, if it was winter, but it's late spring. That fabric is too heavy for this heat. I'm sure it was appropriate for corporate Chicago, but Hastings is more laid-back. Only attorneys wear suits here, and most of them don't wear ties."

Nina clenched her teeth to stop the snippy comment on the tip of her tongue. "Do you usually tell newcomers how to dress when they arrive in town, or is it just me that you're finding fault with? First you hint that I might like to take advantage of the Tranquility Spa, and then decided my shoes were dangerous. Now you're telling me my wardrobe is all wrong. Your hospitality needs some work."

Bret gripped the steering wheel. "I'm sorry. I didn't mean to insult you or suggest that you needed some kind of makeover. You're perfectly fine the way you are."

"Gee, thanks."

"I just meant you'd be more comfortable if you dressed differently. Less fussy and more relaxed." He sighed. "I'm going to shut up now. I'm only making things worse."

"Yes, you are." She regretted snapping at him. After all, he had no idea what she was facing today.

"This is me trying to be helpful. I promised Kitty I'd look out for you, get you settled and make sure you were comfortable. I guess I'm not real sure how to do that."

"Stop trying. I'm fine. Really. I don't need any help."

"Right. Except to get back and forth to work."

She shot him a glance, but when she looked at him, she saw the sly smile and the twinkle in his green eyes, and her irritation vanished. "I'm sorry. I shouldn't be so sensitive. I'm nervous. It's been a long time since I've seen patients."

"You'll be fine. I'm sure it's like riding a bike."

"I hope so. I don't want to let Kathryn down. She's done me a great favor in letting me fill in for her."

"How so?"

She took a moment to gauge how much to

reveal. "My job was eliminated. Her offer was a blessing. I jumped at the chance." Maybe she'd jumped too quickly. "I hadn't expected things to be so different down here."

Hastings wasn't Chicago. There, she'd been able to blend into the crowd and live an invisible existence. Here, her clothes, her hair and her manner made her stick out like a sore thumb. She was used to being a controlled professional, never letting her emotions show, nor allowing herself to feel them. Over the last year, those emotions had started to build up, threatening to rise to the surface, and she feared that when they grew strong enough, they'd explode and consume her. She knew expressing emotions, dealing with grief and loss, was the only healthy way to get through a traumatic experience. Somewhere along the way, she'd become stuck. She couldn't go back, and she was too afraid to move forward.

"And I'm not making things any easier. I promise, I'll keep my opinions to myself from now on."

He really was a nice man. "And I promise, if I have questions, I'll come to you for help."

"Sounds like a good compromise."

In her office, she settled in behind her desk, making sure her patient notes were ready. Dottie reassured her that Mrs. Alexander was a nice lady, who mainly needed someone to listen to and reassure her that she wasn't crazy. Dottie felt sure after Nina saw the first patient, she'd regain her confidence.

Thankfully, Dottie's prediction proved correct. Nina's self-confidence grew after seeing her first patient. However, the second appointment that morning didn't go as well. The patient was unhappy that Kathryn wasn't there. She tried to reassure the gentleman, but he left with obvious doubts about her ability to help, which only added to her anxiety about the Widow's Walk Club that night. If only she could see the women individually, instead of in a group.

After eating a quick lunch she'd had prepared by her hotel's room service to bring with her to work, she was ready to tackle the afternoon. She'd have to find restaurants nearby, because the cost of having a lunch prepared by room service every day was too expensive.

Picking up the mail Dottie had placed on her desk, she scanned the flyer printed on light blue paper. Hastings Military Appreciation Day. The event Bret had mentioned. The flyer urged the tenants in the building to get involved and volunteer. Nina's conscience sparked. Despite her experience with the service, she held great respect for the military.

Maybe there was something she could do to help. Something small that would be helpful but wouldn't get her too deeply involved. Shoving the flyer into her desk drawer, she set the idea aside for her to consider later.

Her next three sessions were uneventful. She doubted she'd done more than hold their place for the time being, but at least she hadn't upset anyone. Nina opened the large file on the widows' therapy group, hoping that reading through it one more time would boost her confidence and give her an idea of what to expect.

Bret appeared in her doorway. "I've come to take you to a party."

The last thing she wanted to do now. The mere thought of meeting a bunch of strangers set her nerves on edge. She shook her head. "I'm not much for parties."

He smiled and came toward her, reaching for her hand. "You can't say no. This is mandatory."

Sweat broke out on her palms. "No. Really, I don't have time."

"But everyone is looking forward to meeting you." He tugged her to her feet.

Reluctantly, she stood and took a step, but the carpet once again snagged her stiletto heel, and she pitched forward. Bret's arms wrapped around her rib cage, but her forward momentum twisted her ankle, leaving her right shoe stuck in the carpet.

A sharp pain lanced up her calf and she cried out.

In one smooth motion, Bret picked her up and carried her to the sofa, and then he knelt down and took her ankle in his hands, gently touching, twisting and probing, examining for any serious damage.

"Where does it hurt?"

"Nowhere now. I think it's all right." She started to tug her foot from his grasp. His touch was doing strange things to her system. His gentleness and concern warmed her heart, but she didn't need the tingles that were shooting up her leg. His head was bowed over her ankle as he checked for injury, and she wondered if his dark brown hair was as soft as it looked. Her cheeks flamed. What had gotten into her?

Bret looked up and smiled. "Looks like no harm was done. See how it does when you stand on it."

He held out his hand, and she slipped hers into it, acutely aware of the warm strength in his touch. Gingerly, she tested her foot. No pain. She grinned. Crisis avoided.

"Good." He retrieved her shoe from the carpet snag and handed it to her. "I still think these shoes are dangerous."

"You may be right."

"So, are you ready for the party?"

Her good mood died. Why couldn't he just leave well enough alone? His gallant rescue didn't change the fact that she didn't want to mingle with a bunch of strangers.

"No. I'm sorry, but I really don't have the time." She turned her back, hunching her shoulders. He'd probably be angry with her.

Bret exhaled a heavy sigh and touched her shoulder lightly. "I didn't mean to pressure you. I wanted everyone to meet you."

Nina's irritation waned at the sincerity in his deep voice. He meant well, and he did have a way of making her feel better, but he had no idea what she was facing. "No. It's not your fault. I need time to adjust. Everything here is so different."

"I suppose we do take a little getting used to."

"Maybe next time." How could she explain that this was a difficult time of year for her, which only added to her stress. She'd hoped the move here would keep her too busy to dwell on the anniversary, but it wasn't. She glanced at her phone. "I have a patient due in a few minutes, so if you'll excuse me…"

He held her gaze a moment, his green eyes probing and filled with compassion. "Sure thing."

She pulled her gaze from his.

He started out of the room. "If you need anything, just ask."

"I will."

Alone, in the quiet of her office, she poured a drink from the watercooler and let the chilled water dampen the heat in her throat. She should never have come to Hastings. Never agreed to fill in for Kathryn. It was much harder than she'd ever expected.

She sank into her desk chair, her gaze landing on the calendar displayed on the corner. Her nerves screamed at the upcoming date. How was she going to get through Friday in her present state? Reaching out, she grabbed the calendar and shoved it deep into the bottom drawer before picking up the next patient file and losing herself in the contents.

Bret marched into his office and closed the door, rubbing the bridge of his nose. He'd messed up again. He'd convinced himself that the shy Nina simply needed a little push to get her out of her shell. It always worked with his daughter Livvy. A little urging and she could move past her reluctance.

Unfortunately, Nina wasn't an eight-year-old child. Pushing her had only upset her and shoved her deeper into her hole. He'd have to find a different approach. He knew behind that rigid exterior was a sweet, vibrant woman longing to get out. Maybe he could get a better read after they rode back and forth to work a few times. People often opened up while driving. He thought about calling Kitty, but his concerns would only make her worry about her friend, and she didn't need that right now.

The bell tone on his cell chimed, and he smiled. His girls were calling. School was out, and they always checked in. He tapped the speaker button. "Hello, princesses. How was school today?"

Livvy spoke first. "Georgie got in trouble."

"No, I didn't."

"Did too. She had to stay in at recess. She pushed Justin Collins down."

"Livvy, it's not nice to tattle on your sister. Georgie, we'll talk about this later."

"Okay. Grandpa is taking us to get art supplies. I have to make a poster."

"Can I make a poster, too?"

"We'll see. You behave for your grandpa until I get home."

"Did you have a nice day, Daddy?"

Bret's heart warmed. His oldest girl was

the nurturer in the family. Always thinking of others. "I did." A memory of holding Nina in his arms flashed into his mind, making him smile. That had been a very nice part of his day. She'd felt so soft and warm in his arms. He shoved the notion aside.

"Will you be home soon, Daddy?"

"No, Georgie, I have to work tonight, but we'll talk when I get home, okay?"

After a few phone kisses and a couple of *love you*s, Bret ended the call and closed his eyes, rubbing them to ease the tiredness. No matter how hard he tried, he couldn't seem to get the hang of working and being a single dad. If it wasn't for Alan, he'd be at the office every night. If the company would turn a profit, he might be able to take on more help, but right now, that was out of the question. They were barely staying afloat.

It was nearly five o'clock when Bret finished preparing for the computer class he would be conducting this evening. He needed to check with Nina about tonight. The widows' group met this evening, and he suspected she planned on taking a cab back to the hotel. Not a good idea.

The door to her office was open when he entered the reception area, which meant she didn't have a patient. He stopped at the doorway of her office. She was deep in concentration, no doubt preparing for her first group therapy session with the widows. He had to admire her diligence.

He tapped on the door frame. She looked up and smiled, causing an unexpected catch in his pulse. She had a beautiful smile. She needed to display it more often. "I just wanted you to know that I have a class tonight, so I can still take you home when you're done."

"Are you sure I won't be putting you out?"

"Not in the least. Knock on my door when you're ready to leave." She nodded, and he tore his gaze from her pretty blue eyes, reminding himself that he had a lousy track record with women. He scolded himself mentally and turned away, making a beeline for his office.

He had to watch himself where his new tenant was concerned. She obviously had issues, and she wasn't like one of his vets, whom he could easily connect with. They had shared experiences. He had no idea what Nina had been through. But something about the woman had latched on to him and he couldn't ignore her.

# Chapter Three

Nina glanced at the clock in her office Tuesday evening, tapping her fingernails on the desktop. The ladies would be here in fifteen minutes, and she was having a full-blown anxiety attack. She'd tried a few deep breathing exercises, several stress-relieving stretches and even resorted to a brief prayer, but nothing helped.

Intellectually, she knew she was prepared for this group therapy session. She'd read the files and all of Kathryn's notes, and she had a pretty good idea of what to expect. Still, the thought of trying to guide a group of widows triggered all her insecurities. No. Her fears. These women could shatter all the windows in her shrine of grief.

The door swooshed open, and a tall blonde woman entered carrying a large purse over her shoulder. She was dressed in skinny jeans that fit the way they'd been intended, and a soft green flowing top. With her long hair and bright green eyes, she looked like she'd stepped off the pages of *Vogue*. She saw Nina and a huge smile brightened her face.

"You must be Nina. Ooh, I'm so glad to meet you. I'm Evelyn Clark." She spread her arms and hurried forward, wrapping Nina in a huge, perfume-laced hug. Thankfully, the awkward moment ended quickly, and she was able to hide her discomfort.

The door opened again, and two more ladies entered. One was a middle-aged woman with salt-and-pepper hair, wearing a simple pair of jeans, plain knit top and tennis shoes. The other woman was close to Nina's age and wore leggings under a long tunic, and large gold earrings that accented her dark curly hair. They introduced themselves as Paula Ingram and Charlotte Kirby. Nina knew the names from her files. Evelyn had lost her hubby to cancer many years ago. Paula's husband had been killed in an oil rig accident in the Gulf. Charlotte was a military wife who lost her husband in the line of duty.

The ladies made their way into her office and got comfortable. Nina took a seat and glanced at the door. Officially, there were eight women in the group, but according to Kathryn's notes, not all of them attended regularly. "How many more are you expecting?"

Evelyn placed her purse on the floor beside her chair. "Jen and Trudy are coming, but Rona has a school thing, and Elise has a migraine."

Nina checked her file. "And what about Yvonne Monroe?"

The women all wore silly smiles. "I don't think she'll be back. She's met someone and it's getting serious. I think we'll hear wedding bells soon."

Nina remembered several notes in Yvonne's file. Her husband had been murdered. Her file was the thickest. She had a long, hard climb back to mental health. It was good she was transitioning forward into a new life, but the thought of doing the same for herself knotted Nina's stomach.

The door opened once more, and two women hurried in. The first was a small woman wearing a simple skirt and blouse and dark-rimmed glasses. The other was plump with graying hair and a cheery smile. Her perfectly tailored linen outfit suggested she was well-off.

"Sorry we're late." The older woman grinned

and hurriedly took a seat. "I'm Jen. And she's Trudy."

Trudy took a seat in one of the side chairs slightly apart from the others, who had gathered on the sofa. Nina made a mental note of this, and then settled in, being sure to make eye contact with each woman and ignore the butterflies in her stomach. "I'm glad to meet you. Kathryn tells me you've been a group for a number of years."

Jen nodded. "We've had some come and go. Several have remarried and are living happily-ever-after."

"Since I'm the new one here, why don't we start by telling me what you usually talk about."

The women shared glances and knowing smiles.

Evelyn spoke first. "Well, actually, we want to get to know you."

Paula leaned forward. "Before we spill our guts, so to speak."

"Don't listen to them." Jen held up a hand. "They're just nosy. Don't tell them a thing."

Nina stifled a smile. She'd been worried, but they all seemed relaxed and made her feel at ease. Even comfortable.

"So, tell us about you." Evelyn clasped her hands together and smiled. "All we know is that you're a widow like us. Kitty wouldn't tell us any more than that."

The warmth faded and turned to icy alarm. They knew. She hadn't planned on sharing that information so soon. Not until she'd grown more comfortable with the women.

Trudy nodded. "We were glad to hear that. You'll be able to share things we haven't experienced yet."

No, she couldn't. How could she when she'd never gone down that road? She didn't understand anything about being a widow. She'd spent the last three years deliberately *not* understanding it.

"How long has it been?"

All five women had their eyes on her, waiting for her answer. She clasped her hands tightly in her lap. "Three years."

Jen sighed softly. "How did it happen?"

*Please don't make me say the words.* "He was killed in Afghanistan."

"I'm so sorry. My husband was a soldier, too. I understand."

Nina expected to feel the searing pain of loss again, but Charlotte's soft tone of understanding scrubbed off the sharp edges she usually encountered. The realization left an uneasy sensation in her chest. "Well, as much as I'd like to spend time getting to know each other, I think it best if we start our session. We only have an hour."

"Well, then I'll go first." Evelyn took a deep breath and smiled. "This is my last meeting. I won't be back."

Mumbles of disbelief traveled around the room.

"Remember that job offer I had in Louisville? Well, I took it. I'm leaving Friday."

The women quickly surrounded their friend and hugged her, expressing their joy.

Evelyn sat back down. "I was so dependent on my husband that, when he died, I was lost. I never believed I could do anything without him. It took me seven years, but here I am, ready to move away from the only home I've ever known and start a new life in a new city. And I'm excited."

"I wish I was as brave as you." Trudy adjusted her glasses. "I could never leave Hastings, let alone Mississippi. I'd be terrified." She looked at Nina. "Were you scared to leave Chicago and come here?"

Caught off guard, Nina searched for a proper response. She was supposed to facilitate this session, not participate in it, but the women expected an answer. "Not really. Though I didn't think about it too much. Kathryn called, and I was able to help, so I came."

Trudy sank back into her chair. "Everyone is braver than me."

Jen reached over and squeezed her hand. "Nonsense. You just need to build your self-confidence."

Paula nodded. "There's nothing wrong with staying in one place your whole life. Remember, Kitty said, we each have a growing trail to walk, and it's different for each of us. It just takes some of us longer to deal with the grief."

"Or not deal." Charlotte spoke up. "I wish I'd faced it sooner. It's been ten years, and I'm only now starting to move forward. What does that say about me?"

Nina listened to the various conversations and the admissions as the women shared their varied journeys down "the widow's walk to wholeness," as Kathryn called it. Before she knew it, the session was over, and she realized her anxiety had been for nothing.

As she lay in bed that night, their comments burrowed into her mind. She'd seen herself in each of the women. Denying the reality, afraid to move forward, feeling lost and inadequate. She'd always believed she was alone in those feelings. Despite knowing the stages of grief and recovery, they never seemed to apply to her, only her patients.

The women were as warm and friendly as

Kathryn had said. The session had gone better than she'd anticipated. It had practically run itself. All she had to do was observe and record, and offer an encouraging word.

Next week she'd be far less anxious about the group. They might even give her more to think about. But she'd have to be more careful about sharing her own story. She wasn't ready for that and probably never would be.

He was running, but his feet weighed a ton, making forward progress difficult. He saw the soldier fall. He shouted, but he was too late. Two soldiers, hands clasped in the dust and debris of the explosion. He'd failed in his mission. He'd vowed to protect the man with his life, but he'd allowed his chaplain to be killed.

Bret sat up in the bed, sweat running down his neck and beading up on his forehead. It had been a long time since he'd had the dream. Months. Why had it resurfaced now?

Sleep now was pointless. He got out of bed and headed to the kitchen for a glass of tea. The house was stuffy, so he opted for the cool darkness of the back porch. A few moments later, the back door opened and his father joined him. Bret willed him to leave, but he knew he wouldn't and that talking about the dream usually helped—some.

"Same old dream or something new?"

"Same."

"How long you plan on nursing this load of guilt?"

"Dad, don't."

"It was an accident. Not your fault. His choice. Not yours."

"My responsibility. My failure. Only two military chaplains killed in battle in the last fifty years, and one of them was mine."

"The army doesn't blame you, and the good Lord has forgiven you, so you must like carrying that weight on your back, or you'd let it go." Dad stood. "Same way you keep blaming yourself for Sylvia walking out. Her fault. Not yours."

Bret set his jaw. His father had no idea the depth of his guilt where his marriage was concerned. He should have seen how unhappy Sylvia was. He should have known that he wasn't pulling his weight.

"Find someone to talk to, son, before this thing eats you alive."

Nina Johnson's face came to mind. Bret had a feeling she would understand. He had no idea what her issue was, but the chain-mail coat she wore around her heart was familiar. If it weren't for his girls, he'd be wearing one as thick and impenetrable as hers. He doubted being so withdrawn was good for a psychologist. She should understand things better than most. Unless she'd been hurt deeper than most. Maybe therapists, like medical doctors, made the worst patients. Too close to the trees to see the forest they were lost in.

He hated the thought of the lovely Nina lost and alone. It was a hard way to live. And for some reason, it was important to him for her to be happy.

It was Friday. Nina ran a hand through her hair and let her gaze travel around Kitty's office. Maybe she should have stayed home today. There were no patients scheduled. Dottie wouldn't be here. Nina could have stayed at the hotel, buried her head beneath the pillow and waited for tomorrow to come. But she'd learned from painful experience that trying to ignore this day only made it longer. It was best to keep busy. She still had dozens of case histories to read over, and after the widows' meeting, she wanted to learn more about each of her ladies.

They were all so strong and confident. She envied their ability to walk through their grief and come out in the later years feeling whole and filled with hope and a sense of purpose. Things she would never experience. But they had fired her curiosity, and some of the things they'd said had forced her to think about her own situation. Which was why she wanted to be better prepared next week. She had to be able to control the discussion and steer it away from herself.

An email popped up on her cell screen, illuminating the time and date. Tears pierced the backs of her eyes. She forced them away. She had to get through today in one piece, and the only way to do that was to work. Hard.

Bret had tried to question her about her withdrawn mood on the way to work, but she'd brushed it off as fatigue from the stressful first week on the job. Thankfully, he remained silent during the rest of the ride. Once there, she'd hurried to the office and pulled an emotional blanket around herself.

Five years ago, this day, she'd lost the most precious thing in her life. Her daughter, Molly. Surviving this day was the hardest thing she faced each year.

The stack of patient files kept her busy through to midafternoon. A box lunch from the hotel had helped her avoid going out to eat. Bret must have had a busy day since he hadn't popped in to check on her. Either that or her cold-shoulder attitude this morning had scared him off. Strangely enough, she was getting used to him watching out for her. It had been a long time since anyone had cared about how she was doing.

She glanced at the clock. In a couple of hours, she could go home, hide under the covers and watch some mindless pay-per-view movie, and when she woke up tomorrow, she could put it all behind her for another year.

"Nina."

She looked up as Bret came through her office door. Her heart lurched when two little girls scurried in behind him.

"I have some people I'd like you to meet."

Caught off guard, she could only stare. *No, please, not now.* She wasn't strong enough to face children today. Tomorrow.

From somewhere far off, she heard his voice as he introduced his children. He touched the top of each little head lovingly as he spoke.

"This is Olivia—she's eight—and this one is Georgiana. She's five."

She recalled Bret mentioning he had two daughters, but she'd ignored it. She didn't want to know about Bret's personal life. The less she knew, the less involved she'd become.

The sight of the older girl plunged a hot knife into her throat. She was the same age as Molly when… The memories she kept locked away came clawing back, and she was powerless to stop them. She gritted her teeth and tried to look pleasant.

The girls said hello, and Georgie waved, a big smile on her sweet little face. "Hello." She wasn't sure she actually made an audible sound, because blood surged loudly in her ears, and her heart thundered so hard her chest hurt. She thought Bret said something about the girls wanting to meet her, but she wasn't sure about that.

"Can we color?" The little one bounced on her toes.

"Miss Kitty keeps books and colors for the children, and sometimes she colors with us. Do you like to color?"

Olivia's question stole her breath. Molly loved to color. She looked at Bret and saw his expression fade from proud parent to friendly smile to deep concern. She should say something. Explain, but her heart was being shredded. The two little girls with their pigtails and sweet smiles were yanking the thick cover from her deeply buried memories. Memories that would consume her if she let them loose.

"Girls, why don't you go back to my office and tell Miss Jackie that I said you can have some cookies. I'll be there in a minute."

"But we just met the pretty lady."

"Go on. Grandpa will be here soon to pick you up."

Nina managed to say goodbye in a calm voice, but the minute the girls were gone, she turned her back and wrapped her arms around her waist.

"Are you all right? I didn't mean to barge in. I get carried away with my girls. I think everyone should find them as adorable as I do. I never considered that you might not like children."

His words sliced through her emotional fog. "I like children."

"Really? Most people smile when they see little kids. You gritted your teeth and went pale as a ghost."

Her conscience pressed like an anvil upon her spirit. She couldn't keep living like this. "I was surprised. That's all. I wasn't expecting to see them today." Tears filled her eyes. She snatched a tissue from the box on her desk, willing herself to stop. Crying would only bring about more questions, and she wasn't in any condition to answer them.

"Nina. What's going on? Is there anything I can do?"

"No. I'm fine. Just go back to work." The sob escaped her throat before she could stop it.

Bret came and took her arm, steered her

toward the sofa and eased her down. He sat beside her. "I'm not leaving until you tell me what's wrong."

"I'm sure your girls need you."

"They'll be fine."

She looked into his eyes and saw concern and compassion. Maybe she should tell him a small part. Then he would leave, and she could regain control. She stared into Bret's green eyes, sensing his gentle urging to confide in him. He was safe. He was trustworthy. She opened her mouth, but nothing came forth. Why was it so hard to say the words? She'd come here hoping the change would allow her to finally start dealing with all the pain and loss. She hadn't expected it to be so terrifying. She looked at Bret still patiently waiting. The bare facts. That was all.

"I had a daughter. She died. Five years ago today."

Bret exhaled a slow breath and bowed his head. "Oh, Nina. I'm so sorry. I had no idea." He rubbed his forehead. "And I chose today to parade two little girls in front of your face. I never would have done that if I'd known."

Speaking the words released the tension on her nerves. "It was a long time ago."

Bret took her hand in both of his, sending a warmth through her veins that chased the chill in her blood away. "But the pain never goes away. Does it?"

How did he know?

"I haven't lost a child, but losing my wife is a pain I'm not sure I'll ever completely overcome. Losing someone you love leaves a big hole inside, and it feels like a cold wind is always blowing through it, reminding you of the emptiness."

His words overrode her ache, replacing it with a strong need to understand. "Yes. It does. What happened?"

"I was a career soldier. She couldn't take the long separations. One day she'd had enough and walked out, leaving the girls with my dad. I was deployed overseas. I took an early discharge and came home."

His admission lodged in her heart, shifting her focus away from her hurt. "I'm so sorry. Raising two little girls alone must be hard." What she wouldn't give to have the chance to raise Molly.

"We do all right. We live with my dad, and he's a big help."

Bret grazed his thumb over the back of her hand. "Who helped you, Nina?"

Nina pulled her gaze from his. "No one."

"Why not?"

She stood and walked to the window. What

was the point of keeping the truth to herself any longer? Bret had pried open the door, so she might as well open it all the way. "Because it was my fault she died. I killed her."

She turned and faced him, bracing for what she would see on his face. His green eyes revealed his shock and disbelief. The muscle in his jaw flexed. How he must hate her now. He'd turn away the same as her husband, Chip, had done.

She blinked away the tears and lifted her chin. "You'd better go. I have more work to do."

She dared a look into his eyes. He started forward, arms outstretched, and she turned away. All she wanted was to be left alone.

"Nina, we should talk about this. Tell me what happened."

"There's nothing to tell. Please. I need to get back to work."

For a moment, she thought he'd refuse. The tenderness in his green eyes was nearly her undoing. She may have only known him for a short while, but it was obvious he was a protector. A fixer, and he'd try to rationalize what happened.

He ran a hand down the back of his neck, clearly reluctant to go. "All right. I'll knock when I'm ready to leave."

She nodded, only drawing a breath when he had closed the door behind him.

Pulling out her phone, she called the cab company. She had to leave now before she completely fell apart. She prayed that the taxi would be punctual this time. She needed to escape and hide from the pain before her heart exploded.

# *Chapter Four*

Nina opened the curtains in her hotel room and gazed out at the picturesque downtown view. It was a beautiful Saturday morning. Flowers and trees bloomed profusely along the sidewalks. She'd been in Hastings a week but had never fully appreciated the charm of the little city. Probably because she'd been too focused on her new job and getting through the anniversary of Molly's death.

She'd cried herself to sleep last night, but unlike years before, her dreams of her daughter weren't dark nightmares, but flashes of happy times, and of Molly's sweet face and her giggle. When she woke up this morning, something was different. The sharp sting of Molly's memory was muted. She could lift out a few special moments and examine them without feeling as if she were suffocating.

The loud ring of her cell jarred her from her thoughts. Dottie's name appeared on the screen, raising a thread of concern. "Hello, Dottie. Is everything all right?"

"Of course. I was just calling to check up on you. Bret told me about yesterday. I thought maybe you could use a friend to talk to."

Apparently, working in a small office building was similar to living in a small town. News traveled fast. "I'm fine."

"Kiddo. Kitty told me about your daughter. Not to be gossiping, but so that I'd be here to lend a hand if you needed it. It must have been hard seeing Bret's girls unexpectedly like that."

Some of the tension left her body. Talking to Dottie would help. "It was. But in a strange way, it freed me up to start looking at Molly's memory with a bit of emotional distance."

"That's good. And you have to admit, Bret's girls are pretty cute with their brown eyes and dark hair."

They were, though not as beautiful as her daughter. "Molly's hair was blond, but she had the same sparkle in her eyes." Bret still had his girls. Hers was gone because of her carelessness. She shook off the thought. She knew it would only lead to depression, and she'd end up locked away in her room like she'd been for the last five years.

"Are you still regretting your move here?"

"What makes you think that?"

"Sweetie, I'm pretty good at reading people, and it's all over you like kudzu on a fence post."

She'd have to do better at hiding her emotions if she was going to keep anything hidden from her new secretary. "Yesterday, I would have said yes. But now I'm thinking coming to Hastings is exactly what I needed."

The professional in her knew she was in denial and avoiding the stages of grief because it would mean moving forward. And that meant letting Molly and, for that matter, her husband, Chip, fade into the background of her life and become nothing more than a sweet musical grace note.

"Good. I think you need to be here as much as we need you to be. You're good for those widows, and you're good for me. Why don't you take the weekend to pamper yourself. Relax, see a movie or go shopping. Treat yourself to a new hairdo. It always does wonders for my state of mind."

She smiled at the motherly tone in Dottie's voice. "Thanks, Dottie. I really appreciate your concern." Dottie urged her to get out and explore the historic town of Hastings before hanging up.

Nina took a sip of her coffee. Dottie was right. Fresh air and a brisk walk would do wonders for her mood. It was time she stopped hiding.

She picked up her brush and pulled it through her hair. Then she reached for the dark headband she usually wore. She halted at the image of herself in the mirror. The woman reflected there was a stranger. She ran her fingers through her shoulder-length hair. The ends were uneven, and the strands dull. When was the last time she'd had it cut, let alone styled? It was easier to slide the headband on and not worry about how her hair looked.

She used to take great care in her appearance and her wardrobe. She used to be vibrant, smiling and energetic. Now she was dull, bland and lifeless. That wasn't who she wanted to be. Maybe starting over meant starting with herself. When was the last time she'd bought a new dress or a pair of jeans? She lived in suits at work and sweatpants and T-shirts at home.

A feeling of lightness and anticipation coursed through her, buoying her spirits. Quickly, she dressed in the only pair of slacks she'd brought, tossed on a simple blouse and shoes with the lowest heels and started down to the lobby. After getting directions to a few stores, she stepped outside and breathed in the warm air, letting the sunshine warm her face. A Bible verse she hadn't thought of in a long time came to mind about rejoicing in the day the Lord had made.

Today she would rejoice.

Bret made the turn onto Liberty Street on Monday morning, trying to ignore the anxiety building inside his chest. He'd spent most of the weekend worrying about Nina. Her revelation about her daughter had knocked him back on his heels. Her claim that the death was her fault had lodged like an arrow inside his heart. Sylvia's abandonment had wounded him to the core, but he could not in a million years ever imagine the pain of losing a child. He doubted he could survive that loss.

It explained a lot about Nina: her reluctance to join in, her desire to be left alone, to rely only on herself. But while he understood it, he also knew it wasn't healthy. Kitty hadn't told him much about her friend. She had mentioned Nina's husband had died. Bret wondered if the losses were connected somehow. It would take an iron woman to survive a double loss like that.

He'd wanted to talk to her more, to get an explanation of how her daughter died and why she blamed herself. But she'd left shortly after their talk. He'd seen the cab pull up in front of the office and whisk her away. He'd have to wait to talk to her later, and he had a feeling she wouldn't be open to any questions.

Mostly, he was worried about her. He wanted to comfort her—as a friend. Give her someone to talk to, to confide in, though he doubted she'd agree to that. Her emotional shield was thick and high.

Pulling the SUV to the curb in front of the hotel, he scanned the people on the sidewalk, looking for the woman in the dark suit. She normally stuck out like a brown pelican in a flock of bright pink flamingos.

When the passenger door opened, and a woman climbed in, it took him a second to realize it was Nina. She looked completely different in a pair of light gray linen slacks under a figure-flattering pale green top. Her hair, freed from the headband, was shorter and floated around her face in soft waves. He searched for words.

"What happened to you?" Inwardly he cringed. He'd sounded accusatory, and that wasn't what he meant to convey. "I'm sorry. That came out wrong."

"I'm getting used to it."

"It's just that you look different. I didn't recognize you."

A small smile moved her lips, putting a light in her blue eyes that he'd never seen before. "You look…" He chose his words carefully. No need to antagonize her. "…like a native."

She laughed, catching him off guard. With a full smile and sparking eyes, she was stunning. His breath lodged in his throat.

"Thank you. I decided to take your advice and buy clothes that were more appropriate for the weather. And you were right. It's much more comfortable without the heavy suit and the heels."

"I never meant to criticize you. I just wanted you to feel at ease."

"I know. And to answer your question, what happened to me was an awakening. I can't explain it, but after telling you about Molly, I went to the hotel to hide until the day was over. I cried myself to sleep like I always do, but when I woke up, I wasn't haunted by the day she died. Instead, I remembered a fun day we had making cupcakes. I don't know what changed, except that telling you about her freed me somehow. I always thought if I let those memories loose, they'd overpower me and I'd die." She sighed and studied her hands. "Silly, huh?"

"Not at all. I'm familiar with the feeling, but I've discovered that memories can't kill you."

"I see that now. Anyway, I decided it was time to do what I came here to do. To start putting the past behind me. I thought starting with my appearance would be a not-too-scary way to begin."

"I approve. You look great."

"Because before I looked awful?"

Bret exhaled. He could never seem to say the right things with this woman. "No. I mean you look approachable, friendly and not…"

"Not like a crossing guard with her hand out, telling everyone to stop and stay back?"

The twinkle in her eye eased his tension. "Yeah. Something like that."

She smiled and turned her face to the window. They rode the rest of the way in silence, until he parked the vehicle behind the office. He wanted to know more. He had so many unanswered questions. "Why do you blame yourself for your daughter's death?"

The wary look returned to her blue eyes, turning them to a dull gray. "Because it was." She opened the door to get out, but he took her arm.

"Nina, I'm a good listener, and I don't share what I learn with anyone."

"I know. But despite the change in my appearance, I'm not ready to bare my soul."

He nodded. "Okay. I understand. But just so you know, when you're ready, I'm here to help."

She paused and the blue returned to her eyes. "Well, I could use your help with one thing."

"Name it."

"I need to find a place to live. I can't afford to stay in the hotel much longer. I'll have to find a place close so I can walk to the office."

"That might not be so easy. Our building is in a nice part of town, but I don't think there are any apartments nearby. Maybe you could rent a house. That still doesn't solve the problem of transportation. May I ask why you don't drive?"

"I have my reasons."

Her guard had gone up again. Maybe one day she'd feel safe enough to confide in him. "Then we'll start looking for a place near the office. I'll ask around."

"Thank you. I've already contacted a rental agent, but he's not very interested in finding a place for only a few months."

"All right, but at least let me drive you

around to look at places. I feel responsible, and I want to make sure it's in a good part of town."

"You're not responsible for me."

"Kitty told me I was. I promised her. Besides, I know the area. You don't."

"All right. Thank you."

Bret slid out of the vehicle and went around to Nina's door, feeling a sense of accomplishment. Finally there was something he could do to help Nina. The best part was, she'd asked him, and he wouldn't stop until he'd found the perfect place for her to stay.

Nina munched the last bite of her pasta salad, and then tossed the remains into the trash. It was Tuesday again, and the widows were due soon for their session. Time had gone so fast, she found it hard to believe that this was her third meeting with the women. Last week, the ladies had been delighted over the changes she'd made in her appearance, complimenting her on the new hairstyle and the casual clothes. She'd admitted that her motivation was based partly on wanting to fit into her new environment. Thankfully, her comment had sparked a response from Trudy, who opened up and shared her deep fears about being different and how being a widow caused some of her friends and family to pull away when she needed them most. Nina understood completely. People were awkward and uncomfortable and at a loss for what to say, or how to comfort. It was easier to stay away.

She found herself making comparisons to her own situation. After Molly's death, her mother had blamed her for the accident. Chip had tried to comfort her, but he was hurting equally, and Nina knew, deep inside, he blamed her, too. When he suddenly announced he was reactivating his military service, she knew in her heart it was his way of running away from her.

Chip's abandonment had caused her to withdraw behind an impenetrable wall. Now the barrier was starting to crumble, and she was seeing things in a new light. Hearing the widows share their journeys had helped her realize how deeply stuck she actually was, and it wasn't healthy.

Out in the reception area, Nina sat down at Dottie's desk and opened the patient file she'd left there only to be distracted by a slight movement of the office door. She looked up to see a little face appear. She smiled. "Hello, Olivia. That's your name, right?"

She nodded. "Are you feeling better?"

"What do you mean?"

"Daddy said you were feeling bad when we were here before. He said that's why you didn't talk to us."

Nina's throat clenched. She hadn't considered how her reaction might have appeared to the little girls. "Oh. Yes, that's true." The door pushed open farther and another sweet face appeared.

"Let me in. I want to see her, too." Georgie ducked under her sister's arm. "Hi. Are you all better now?"

"Much better. Thank you for asking."

Georgie's eyes lit up. "Can we color now?"

"Oh. I'm sorry, but I don't have any books or colors here."

Olivia entered and headed for the tall armoire against the wall. "Yes, you do. Right here." She pulled out a drawer and held up a stack of books and a big box of colors.

Bret suddenly strode into the room and glared at his daughters. "What are you doing in here? I told you to stay in my office." He cast an apologetic glance in her direction. "I'm sorry. They usually mind better than this. I hope they haven't upset you."

"No, not at all." She had to smile at the cute little girls. "They were just wondering if I was feeling better."

Bret rubbed a hand over his chin. "Oh,

yeah, I had to tell them something. They wouldn't understand what was really upsetting you that day."

"It's all right."

"Let's go, kiddos. Back to my office. Miss Nina has work to do."

"But we want to color."

"Why don't you each take a book and a box of crayons with you. You can bring them back later."

"Can we, Daddy?"

"Sure. But get going." He gestured toward the door. The girls waved and said goodbye as they hurried out the door.

Georgie blew her a kiss. "I'm glad you're feeling better."

Bret stopped in the doorway. "I'm sorry about this. It won't happen again."

"It's all right. They are welcome to visit anytime. Actually, I'm glad they came. It gives me a chance to thank you for being so understanding the other day. I should have said so sooner."

The small smile on his face and the tender light in his eyes sent a tingle along her nerves. "You're welcome. That's what friends are for."

As the door closed behind him, Nina found herself liking the idea of having Bret for a friend.

The girls' visit had left a warm spot under her breastbone. Their concern for her was so very sweet. A quick check of the clock reminded her that her widows' session would be starting any moment. Quickly, she tidied up the office and collected her notes in time to see the door swing open and Paula step in. "Good evening."

She smiled and dropped her purse beside the flowered armchair. Her usual spot. "How's the apartment hunt coming?"

Nina rose and walked to the chair that she'd dubbed her director's chair and laid her notepad down. "Not well. There are no apartments close enough for me to walk to work, and even if I could find one on a bus line or arranged for transportation, they all want a year's lease. I won't be here that long."

Paula made a sour face. "You don't want to ride the bus, trust me. How about renting a room or a small house?"

"I've been working with a real-estate agent, but she's about ready to dump me. She can't understand why I don't drive."

"It does complicate things. I'd be lost without my car. Maybe it's time you started driving again."

"No." She'd spoken too quickly and forcefully. Paula's eyes widened in surprise. "That's not an option. Something will turn up. I can't rely on Bret to keep bringing me back and forth to work."

"Oh?" Her tone oozed curiosity. "I wouldn't mind him taking me anywhere anytime." She waved a hand in front of her face like a fan. "He's one handsome hunk, that one."

Nina grinned and shook her head. "Kathryn asked him to look after me, that's all. He's been very kind, but I can't keep imposing."

"Kind, huh? Maybe there's more to his looking after you than you think?"

The idea held more appeal than it should have. She shoved it aside. "Hardly. I'm not the type men are drawn to."

"You don't really believe that, do you?"

Jen and Charlotte entered the room, and Paula turned her attention to them. "Hey, Nina doesn't think she's the type men are attracted to."

"That's not what I said."

The women exchanged looks before taking their seats. Jen's eyes widened as if she'd been told something shocking. "That's crazy. She's adorable."

Paula pointed and nodded. "There. See. I told you."

Their sweet compliments and support warmed every corner of Nina's being, even though having the focus on her made her uncomfortable. "We're not here to talk about me. Let's get started. We'll be a small group tonight. Just the four of us. Who'd like to start?"

Jen leaned forward, hands tightly clasped. "I want to let go."

"Of what?"

"All of it. The pain, the guilt, the fear, the sadness. I want to move on, but I'm stuck. I thought I was okay, but I realize all I've been doing is rearranging the emotions. Not confronting them."

A shiver chased down Nina's spine. She could have spoken those words. She forced herself to focus on Jen. "What scares you the most? Start there."

Jen took a few moments to collect her thoughts. "Letting go of the grief. If I let go, then it'll be like deleting him from my life as if he never mattered. He did matter. He was important. And I promised him I'd never love anyone but him."

Charlotte reached over and took her hand. "Oh, sweetie, you can't base your future on a promise made years ago. If you really love someone, you don't wish them a life of loneliness. That's selfish and cruel. You'd want them to be happy."

Nina wouldn't have phrased things in that

way, but Charlotte had a point. "Jen, if he were the one left behind, would you want him to stay single and be alone?"

She wiped tears. "No. I wouldn't."

Paula came and gave Jen a hug. "You deserve to be happy."

Nina agreed. "Letting go of the grief doesn't mean you're forgetting or downplaying the importance of your life with your husband."

"If your old man is in heaven, then he's too busy praising the Lord to be wondering what you're doin' down here."

Nina chuckled along with the others. Leave it to Paula to be blunt.

Jen wiped her eyes and smiled. "So, I won't be a horrible person if I let go of the past?"

A chorus of reassuring comments floated in the room. Nina scanned each woman's face. The affection they held for one another, the genuine support, was wonderful to see. She envied them this relationship.

Once again, the session had revealed a truth she'd been avoiding. Moving beyond her grief wasn't a shameful thing. It was a normal part of living a full life. Maybe someday she'd believe that completely.

Bret hung up the phone and leaned back in his chair. Finally, a breakthrough in his search for a nearby apartment for Nina. He'd become as frustrated as she was trying to find something. But in a suburban city like Hastings, walkable wasn't an option. Everyone here drove a car. He'd added that to his Nina to-do list. First was to find her a place to live; second was to convince her to drive again.

Thankfully, he may have solved problem number one, and he couldn't wait to tell Nina. Unfortunately, her office door was closed, which meant she was with a patient, so his potential good news would have to wait.

It was almost quitting time when Alan walked into his office.

"How'd the chamber meeting go last night? Did they like your idea about making it more of a family event?"

Bret rubbed his forehead. "They liked it fine, but their ideas didn't go beyond balloons for the kids and face painting."

Alan perched on the edge of Bret's desk. "Yeah, that'll bring in the crowds, all right."

"I doubt if even Olivia and Georgie would find that exciting."

"Find what exciting?"

Bret's pulse did a funny skip at the sound of Nina's voice. "Hey. What brings you into our humble domain?"

"I just wanted to let you know that I'm

ready to leave whenever you are. I was going to ask you if…"

She stopped, staring at Alan's leg. Perched as he was on the edge of the desk, his prosthetic leg was exposed beneath his pants.

Alan chuckled softly and hiked the trouser up a little more. "Ain't it pretty?"

Nina blushed and lowered her gaze. "I'm sorry. I didn't mean to stare. I didn't know you had… I mean, I didn't realize…"

Alan stood and waved off her concern. "Don't worry about it. It's just a part of who I am these days, thanks to an IED. It could have been worse. I've come to love the bionic leg. I can jump higher and run faster, just like that old TV show."

Nina smiled, but Bret could see she was still uncomfortable and filled with questions. He smiled over at her. "It's okay to ask questions."

"Sure. Ask away."

"Oh, no. That would be rude."

"Not at all. I like to talk about it and show people what I can do. The more they understand about prosthetics, the less awkward for everyone."

Nina brushed her hair behind her ears. "So, what were you talking about when I came in that wasn't very exciting?"

"Next month is the annual Military Appreciation Day. They hold it in the city park, on the river. Phase II always participates, but the turnout hasn't been what we'd like. I'm trying to convince the chamber of commerce to beef it up and add more than tents filled with people handing out flyers. We need more activities. Most of the big draws happen at the airport on Veterans Day. They haul out the choppers and the Humvees and all that flashy stuff, but there should be something we can do on a smaller scale to get folks to come out. Something geared more for families."

Nina nodded thoughtfully. "Like bouncy houses and puppies."

"Exactly."

"Hey, this woman has game." Alan laughed.

A wistful look softened Nina's face. "My daughter loved those things."

"My girls would climb a mountain if they knew there were puppies at the top." Bret took her arm and steered her out the door. "We need to do some serious brainstorming on the way home. Plus, I have a surprise for you."

He couldn't wait to tell Nina the good news and hopefully get another glimpse of her dazzling smile.

Settled in Bret's SUV a few minutes later, Nina didn't wait for him to start the conversation. "So, what's the surprise?"

He started the engine, and then he shifted his body so he could face her. "I may have found you a place to live."

"Really? What about a deposit? Do I have to sign a long-term lease?"

He grinned and shook his head. "No. None of that. One of the veterans that comes to Phase II is a contractor, and he's remodeling an old house near here and turning it into four apartments. One of them is completed, and he's finishing up the others, but they won't be done for several months. He's willing to rent you the completed apartment on a monthly basis, with no down payment or lease."

"It sounds perfect. When can I see it?"

"Right now. Ted is waiting for us."

Bret took a moment to appreciate Nina's glowing smile. He liked seeing her happy, and he liked even more that he was the cause. "I really liked your ideas earlier about the Military Appreciation Day."

"I used to help with family-day events at my old church."

"I don't suppose you'd consider helping us out on the event? We're always looking for volunteers, and we could use someone with imagination and experience."

He was surprised to see a shadow pass across her blue eyes, dimming her happiness.

Maybe she really did have something against veterans. He hoped not.

"I'll think about it."

Bret pulled up to the curb in front of the redbrick Foursquare house on Maple Avenue. "Well, here it is."

Nina leaned closer to the window. "It's charming. I love the big front porch."

Ted met them inside the front hall and shook his hand. Dust floated in the afternoon light, scraps of lumber littered the floor and drywall leaned against one wall. "Don't worry about the mess. You must be Nina. I'm Ted Hall."

"I appreciate you letting me stay here. It'll only be for a few months."

"That'll work out fine. I should be done with the other units by then and ready to rent them out." He stepped to one side and opened the door on the right. "This is the finished apartment."

Bret followed her in. Nina was captivated from the moment she stepped inside, exclaiming in delight about the sunny living room, the cozy and efficient kitchen, and the ample space in the bedroom and bath. After the tour, they settled the financial details, and then headed to the hotel.

Nina rested a hand on his forearm, sending a warm rush along his nerves.

"Thank you for finding me a place. It'll be nice to have my own home again."

Her sweet compliment made him feel like a superhero. "It's a nice neighborhood. Safe. I won't worry about you walking back and forth."

"I appreciate your concern, but I'll be fine."

"I have one condition on that. Tuesday nights, I'll still drive you home after the widows' sessions." He braced for her resistance until a smile lit her face.

"Okay."

"And will you think about helping with our event?"

"How could I refuse? You've been such a help to me, driving me back and forth to work, and now finding me a place to live. I'd be happy to help."

Bret reached over and squeezed her hand. "Thanks. I think you're just what we need to elevate this event into something that will draw the crowds."

# Chapter Five

Bret tugged the pink tutu downward while Georgie steadied herself by holding on to his shoulders. "How did dance class go today?"

"Good. We learned to do a position. Watch." She stepped out of the tutu and struck a pose. Bret smiled. She was his enthusiastic daughter. Excited about everything and eager to try anything. Her older sister was more thoughtful and cautious. He marveled at times how the girls could be so different. "That looks hard to do."

Georgie shook her head. "Nope. It's easy."

Bret hung up the tutu and tossed the pink tights into the hamper. "Get dressed. It's almost time for supper. Grandpa made chicken and noodles tonight. Your favorite."

"I hope he makes it for my birthday, too. It's tomorrow, Daddy. You won't forget, will you?"

"It's next month, sweetie, and of course not. How could I forget such an important date?" Not to mention the big red circle on the calendar, and her constant reminders that her big day was coming soon. "But you still have a long time to wait."

She pointed a finger at him, her sweet face held in a stern expression. "Remember, I want a princess dress, a book about bugs and a puppy. With spots."

"I won't forget."

Downstairs, Bret joined his dad in the kitchen to help. "Would you mind if I borrowed your truck this weekend?"

"What for?"

"A friend is moving into her apartment. I offered to loan her that extra bed we have upstairs and a few other pieces of furniture."

Dad stopped and pinned him with a glare. "Is this for that lady friend of yours at work? She seems to be taking up a whole lot of your time. Not to mention forcing you to drive miles out of your way twice a day and waste gas."

"It's my money to spend, so stop worrying about it. Besides, once she's moved in, she'll be walking to work."

"Good. I don't like seeing my son taken advantage of."

"She's not. I'm doing it willingly. Kitty asked me to look after her, and I promised I would. She's new to the city and the South. It's been a kind of culture shock for her. I like her. She's a nice lady."

"So why haven't we met her? You afraid to let the family meet her, or are you ashamed of us? Doesn't she like kids or dogs or old men?"

"Dad, you're being ridiculous. Fine. I'll invite her over for dinner one night."

A sly smile spread over his dad's face. "Good. I want to get a look at her."

Bret exhaled an irritated breath. He should have known. All that complaining was his way of getting to meet Nina. He had to admit, he'd wanted his dad to meet her. The girls had asked about her several times. "Then why don't you help me on Saturday. Then you can meet her for yourself."

"Fine. Saturday it is. I'll get a babysitter for the girls."

The girls darted into the kitchen as the timer dinged on the noodles. It was Bret's favorite time of day. The family gathered around the table, his girls at his side. He loved listening to their sweet chatter. He would never understand how their mother could walk away from these two little princesses. The only explanation was that he'd been a lousy husband.

He couldn't begin to imagine what Nina had gone through losing her daughter. The thought sliced a tiny piece of his heart away. A flicker of doubt rose. Maybe Nina wouldn't want to spend time with his family. It would only point up what she didn't have any longer. He couldn't forget her initial reaction to seeing his girls that day.

Yet she'd claimed the incident had actually helped her to start healing. And she'd been sweet to them the other day, when they came to check on her. *All things work together for good*. Was Nina a believer? That was one qualification that he'd look for if he ever considered marrying again.

Marriage? No. He was not going there ever again.

Nina smoothed the skirt on her print dress, questioning her decision one more time. She was going to a Sunday cookout at the Sinclairs'. Bret had told her to dress casual, but she wanted to make a good impression. She had no idea why. She'd chosen this dress because it was simple and sporty. A nice compromise. She stared at her reflection in the mirror. Why was she acting like a schoolgirl on a first date?

The move yesterday had gone like clockwork. Bret and his dad had delivered a bed frame and mattress, a chest of drawers, and a table and chairs. Dottie and her husband had donated a barely used sofa and chair, along with end tables, a coffee table and an area rug. Dottie had told her about a rent-to-own company where she could get appliances, and they had delivered the stove, refrigerator and a flat-screen TV and installed them.

Everything was done by early afternoon, and she'd spent the rest of the day decorating and "nesting," as Dottie called it. She'd slept like a child her first night in her apartment and awoke feeling more relaxed than she had in a long time. So much so that the pealing of church bells drew her to attend services at a historic church at the end of the street. She'd been hearing God's quiet voice beckoning her back to His side for a while, but there were years of anger and resentment to dig through first.

Her cell phone rang, and she smiled at the name on the screen. Dottie again. She'd called a couple of times last evening to make sure she was okay and had everything she needed. It was nice to have someone looking out for her. She'd been fighting her battles alone for a long time. "Good morning, Dottie."

"I was hoping you'd be awake. I know it's

short notice, but I was wondering if you'd like to attend church with us this morning."

"That's very kind, but I've already attended services at the old church up the street. The bells woke me this morning and invited me."

"That's good. So, do you have plans for today, or are you going to just relax in your new place?"

"That was my original plan." A bubble of excitement formed inside. Being able to retreat to the quiet solitude of her own home after work would be wonderful. She looked forward to all the alone time.

"Don't go hiding yourself away now. That's not good for your frame of mind."

"Actually, I'm going to a cookout at Bret's. He should be picking me up any moment."

"Oh? That sounds interesting. What brought that on?"

"His dad actually invited me. He said it was to celebrate my new place. He and Bret were such a big help yesterday, I could hardly refuse." But at the moment, her anxiety level was swelling. The thought of spending the day with Bret's family made her nervous. She'd prefer to keep their relationship on a simple business-friend level. Anything more hinted at something more serious, and she was not ready for that. Never would be.

"Go and have a good time and watch out for Walt."

That was an odd thing to say. "What do you mean?"

Dottie chuckled. "'Bye, now. I'll talk to you tomorrow."

Thanks to her secretary's concern, Nina's nervousness had eased.

After checking herself in the mirror one last time, she went to the living room to wait for Bret. She smiled and gently touched the framed photo of her and Chip on the bookshelf. It was a sign of the progress she was making that she'd pulled out long-buried pictures of Molly and of her husband. Coming to Hastings, she had finally moved forward, where seeing their images didn't drive a stake through her heart. Her stay here was giving her the strength and courage to go back home and start a new life.

It was why she'd agreed to work with the veterans' event, though she had mixed emotions about that. The military had lured her husband back into battle. The military had gotten him killed. No. That was an easy excuse. Chip had been eager to go overseas. He said it was because he was needed, that it would help him realign his perspective on things. But she knew the truth. He'd wanted to get as far away from her as possible, because being near her only reminded him every minute of who was responsible for their child's death.

Nina shook off the morbid thoughts. They never did any good and only made her feel small and useless. She had to look forward to the future and not dwell in the past. She'd told her widows that very thing this past Tuesday. She needed to apply it to herself.

An unusual sense of excitement took hold when she saw Bret's car pull up out front. A ripple of giddiness zinged along her nerves, making her smile. Of course it was a simple case of nerves. She refused to think she might be attracted to him. It was nothing more than a woman's normal appreciation for a handsome man. Besides, Bret was looking for someone responsible to nurture his girls, not a woman who failed to protect her own child.

Bret took the porch steps quickly, and then he knocked on Nina's door. His gaze scanned the neighborhood as he waited. He hadn't realized a place like this still existed in Hastings. It was a pocket of quiet and charm from another era, with the all modern conveniences only a few blocks away from the office. Nina would be safe here. He wouldn't worry about her walking alone or being cut off from things she needed. But his passenger seat would be awfully empty from now on. He'd gotten used to having her beside him. True, she worked right across the hall and he could see her as much and as often as he pleased, but he'd come to appreciate the intimacy of the SUV.

The door opened, and Bret's heart galloped at the sight of her. She wore a simple print dress that matched her blue eyes and high-lighted her peaches-and-cream skin. Her au-burn hair was free around her shoulders.

"Come on in. I'll be ready in a moment."

He stepped inside, clearing his throat be-fore speaking. "There's no hurry." Was that his voice? He sounded like a squeaky teen-ager. Nina disappeared into the other room, and Bret took the time to scan the apartment. It looked nothing like when he'd left yester-day. The place was completely decorated. Pat-terned curtains hung on the windows, a plush carpet covered the living-area floor and dec-orative knickknacks were displayed on vari-ous surfaces. She'd even hung pictures on the walls. It must have taken her all night to get this place in order. But it was worth it. The apartment had a homey, welcoming feel that couldn't be missed.

A pair of framed photos on the shelving beside the fireplace drew his attention. The first was a picture of a little blonde girl about Livvy's age. Molly. She'd had her mother's smile, but her eyes were darker. Perhaps she took after her father. He glanced at the other photo and paused. It was a picture of a man and a woman, arms around each other's waists, smiling at the camera. He recognized Nina—younger and with much longer hair, but it was the man who captured his attention. He lifted the frame from the shelf to get a closer look. His breath caught when he realized who it was. But how could this be? It was impossible. There had to be some mistake. A brother, maybe, or a cousin? He knew that face. But he couldn't understand why the man was with Nina.

Bret swallowed past the tightness in his throat. "Nina? Is this your husband in the photo?"

"Yes. That's Chip."

She'd answered him from the other room, but he heard her walk into the living area. "Chip?" That wasn't the name he knew the man by. Maybe it was simply a stunning resemblance to the man he knew.

Nina stopped at his side. "His real name was Norman Aloysius Grant, the Third, but his family called him Chip."

Norm. Chaplain Norman Grant. "Grant?"

"I went back to my maiden name after he passed."

Bret fought the scream building inside his chest. He couldn't let on that he recognized her husband. He couldn't explain it to her. Not yet. Maybe never. He had to maintain his composure for now and sort it all out later. Maybe he was wrong.

"What happened to him?" His voice sounded raspy to his ears.

Nina stiffened beside him. "He died. In the war." She turned and walked away, and then she picked up her purse. "I'm ready."

Inside the car, he tried to hide his anxiety. Making trivial conversation would be impossible, so he feigned curiosity about what had happened after he and his father left her apartment yesterday. Thankfully, Nina filled him in with great detail. Her happiness penetrated some of his shock. He was glad she was satisfied with her new place and enjoying making a home again. He'd always suspected that behind her cool, detached facade beat the heart of a homebody. He was relieved when he pulled to a stop in his driveway. Between his dad and his little girls, he wouldn't have to generate much conversation, and that would give him a chance to come to terms with his new discovery.

The chaplain he failed to save was Nina's husband. How could he ever explain it to her? And how was he supposed to live with this new knowledge?

Even more condemning was the fact that Norm had spoken of his wife in such glowing, loving terms, Bret had become intrigued. Too intrigued. He'd finally had to stop listening when the chaplain spoke of his wife. Bret was a married man. His marriage might be rocky, but that was no reason to develop feelings for another man's wife.

*Lord, help me.* How was he going to get through the day? How could he look her in the eyes knowing the truth? His chest hurt. Every nerve in his body was on fire. Guilt lay like an anvil on his spirit.

The front door flew open as they topped the porch steps. Livvy and Georgie scurried out, followed by the dogs, Hank and Daisy. He saw Nina brace herself, but he didn't know if it was because of the dogs or the girls. Her first encounter with his daughters had been difficult. Maybe it still would be. He hadn't considered that when he'd invited her—or rather, his father had.

"I hope you like dogs. I forgot to mention we had a couple."

Nina glanced up at him. "I do."

"We didn't think you'd ever get here." Georgie took hold of Nina's hand.

The animals trotted toward her, stopping and giving her the once-over. The silver German shepherd sat down politely, as if waiting to be introduced. The brown mutt sniffed Nina's fingertips, as if impatient to get acquainted. Bret pushed the animal back and gave it the command to sit, which it ignored.

"The critters here mind about as well as my children."

"This one is mine. Her name is Daisy." Livvy scratched the head of the furry brown mutt lovingly.

"And this one is Hank. He's Grampy's dog." Hank let out a sharp bark, and Georgie smiled happily. "He likes you."

"Give her a chance to catch her breath, Georgie, and say hello to Gramps."

"Okay. But hurry up." She spun and raced back inside, shouting out loud that the Nina lady was here.

Livvy remained on the porch and gave her father an irritated look. "She's so rude."

Bret waved off her concern. "She's just excited."

Olivia took Nina's hand, and Bret stole a quick look at the woman's face. She was smiling, sort of. He wasn't sure how to interpret her expression. Should he rescue her or leave her alone?

Georgie joined them in the hallway, smiling up at Nina. "Do you want to see my room? I have lots of stuffed animals."

"Georgie, Miss Nina doesn't want to see your fake pets." Olivia rolled her eyes and looked at Nina. "She thinks they're real animals."

"They are. And I love them." She sent an angry glare in her sister's direction, and then looked at Nina again. "But I'm going to have a real dog of my own soon, huh, Daddy?"

"We'll see, Georgie."

"It's my birthday soon, and I want a princess dress, a book about bugs and a spotted dog, 'cause I'm going to name her Spotty. So there, you dumb Olivia." She stuck her tongue out at her sister.

Livvy pursed her lips together. "Make her stop doing that."

"Georgie. That's enough. Now run along and play. Miss Nina will be here all afternoon. You'll have plenty of time to spend with her and show her your things."

Bret smiled at Nina as they made their way to the back of the house. "You know how it is with kids. Never a dull moment." He regretted the words the moment they were spoken. How thoughtless could one man be? He caught her gaze as they entered the kitchen, but again, he couldn't read her expression. He couldn't tell if his words had upset her or not. "Sorry for the crazy welcome. I'm so used to the kids and the dogs, I didn't think to warn you."

Her blue eyes softened. "No. I wasn't expecting it, but it was sweet."

The softness faded, and her eyes became shadowed again, as if she only allowed herself fleeting moments of joy.

She held his gaze. "Something smells wonderful."

"Dad is a master grill man." He rested his hand on the small of her back, urging her toward the back door. The contact was light, barely touching, but a steady flow of heat spread through his body. There was no denying his attraction to this woman. But he had to shut that down. Knowing who she was made her off-limits. The last woman on earth he should be interested in.

He glanced at the clock on the kitchen wall as they passed. It was going to be a very long afternoon of tiptoeing on eggshells.

Nina took a fortifying breath as she followed her host through the house. It was a vain attempt to soothe her nerves that had failed miserably. She'd already met the girls at the office and his dad yesterday when they had delivered the furniture. But sharing a family meal was a different situation altogether. She'd have to answer questions, make small talk and be on display. Those were not her strongest qualities. On the other hand, she had to admit that she had an intense curiosity about Bret's home life. He spoke so lovingly of his girls, she looked forward to seeing him interact with them. Walt Sinclair was a sweet, if somewhat ornery, man, who liked to tease. She wondered how much like Bret he was and if his son had a tendency to tease, as well. Bret was usually serious at the office. Friendly but clearly focused on his business.

She hoped to find out more about the veterans' event today, also. She was having second thoughts about participating. Bret had seen Chip's photo, but thankfully hadn't pressed her for more information. That was not a topic she wanted to delve into.

Her gaze took in the cozy charm of the home as they headed toward the back. "You have a lovely home."

"Thanks, but I doubt if it'll ever be featured on HGTV. Dad and I do our best to keep the clutter under control, but the girls make new messes as fast as we can clean up the old ones."

"But isn't that what a home is supposed to be? Lived in and welcoming. Not staged like a magazine photo."

Bret held her gaze. "I suppose so."

Nina stepped out onto the sprawling deck behind Bret's home, a pang of sadness forming beneath her breastbone. She'd had a home like this once. She bit her lip when she remembered she'd never have that again.

Walt was manning the grill at the far end of the deck when she stepped onto the wooden surface.

"Well, it's about time you stopped lollygagging and got out here. Bret, get those hot dogs out here so I can get them started. The burgers are almost done. Miss Nina, I hope you like grilled food. I decided it was too nice a day to fix a heavy sit-down meal inside."

"I love grilling out. Is there anything I can do to help?"

"Nope. Today, you're company. Next time, come prepared to work." He gestured toward the narrow table where beverages had been put out. "Help yourself to a drink and have a seat."

She fixed a glass of lemonade, and then took a seat in one of the comfy chairs at the outdoor table. Getting to know Walt would be interesting. The man was a character.

"So, what do you think of my boy?"

The sip of liquid she'd just taken went down crooked. She coughed a few times. How was she supposed to answer that question? She chose her words carefully. "He's a nice man. He's been very helpful."

"Good-looking kid, isn't he?"

Was Bret's dad playing matchmaker? He'd picked the wrong woman for that. She'd be lying if she told him she didn't find Bret attractive, but she didn't want to encourage the old coot either. "He's a nice-looking man."

"Nice-looking? Ha. He's a hunk."

"Dad!" Bret held the plate of hot dogs, which, at the moment, matched the color of his face. Pink.

Nina wanted to laugh, but she didn't want to embarrass her host any more than he already was.

He handed the plate to his father with more force than necessary. "Stop it. Right now."

Walt harrumphed and glanced over his shoulder at Nina. "My son can't seem to find a nice girl on his own, so I'm going to help him out."

Thankfully, Bret was spared further embarrassment when Walt turned his attention to the food on the grill.

The rest of the afternoon passed quickly, and Nina enjoyed the visit. Walt had stopped his clumsy attempts at matchmaking, and the girls had captivated her with their cute ways. But the old longing in her heart peeked out every now and then, bringing a hunger to be part of a family again. Bret was lucky, despite losing his wife. He had his girls and his dad to sustain him. How wonderful would it be to have a real family again? People to cook for, to care for, a home to surround them and love to give them a reason to get up each morning?

Being here surrounded by Bret's family was stirring up conflicting emotions. The atmosphere was soothing, but seeing the girls only pointed out how much of Molly's life she'd never experience.

A lump lodged in the middle of her chest as she watched Bret pick up Georgie and swing her around. She couldn't take any more. It was too hard. She'd left her purse inside. Maybe she could slip away and call a cab. She shoved her chair back and stood.

"Can you come see my room now?"

Georgie tugged on Nina's hand. The bright smile melted her insides. She had to admire the little one's determination. "I'd love to."

Olivia appeared behind her sister. "Mine first. I'm the oldest."

"No. Mine."

"Girls, it doesn't matter. Miss Nina will see both rooms." Bret's firm tone shut down the argument.

Nina followed them up the stairs, and Livvy tugged her into her room first.

"Daddy just redecorated it for me. I picked out all the colors myself."

The room looked like a rainbow had exploded. Bright blues, yellows and greens yanked the eye in all directions at once. "You must love color. This is amazing."

"I love all colors. I don't have a favorite, so I made every piece a special color. I want to be an artist when I grow up, like my grandmother was."

"I think you'll make an excellent one."

"My turn. Come on."

Georgie darted out the door, and Nina followed to the room across the hall, where the room set a different tone altogether. It was a study in shades of lavender, but very tastefully done.

"Let me guess." She smiled at Georgie. "You love purple."

"Yes, ma'am. I even have a purple dog. See." She scrambled onto her bed, which was covered in a variety of stuffed animals, and held up a deep purple dog with a yellow bow around its neck.

"He's very handsome."

"I know. Sit down, and I'll show you the others."

"Georgie, that'll take forever." Livvy exhaled a loud, exasperated sigh. "She doesn't want to meet all your silly animals."

"Yes, she does. Don't you?"

"Of course."

"See. She likes little kids." Georgie looked up at her with an earnest expression. "Do you have any little kids?"

"Georgiana."

Nina inhaled sharply, caught off guard by the innocent inquiry. Bret's deep voice prevented her from responding. He stood in the doorway, his expression full of sympathy and apology. He had one arm across Livvy's shoulders. The older girl looked embarrassed.

"No, it's all right. I did have a little girl, but I lost her."

"Our mom got lost, too."

"Georgie, Gramps needs your help downstairs."

The little girl must have understood the tone in her father's voice because she scooted off the bed and started from the room before turning and giving Nina a wave. The gesture was so sweet and genuine, tears stung the backs of her eyes.

Bret came and sat beside her on the bed. "I'm so sorry. They don't understand about asking questions that are too personal."

"I know. It's all right." She scanned the room. "Molly would have loved this room. We were in the process of redecorating when…" She stood, suddenly too aware of Bret's nearness and the wave of compassion emanating from him. He was a warm and caring man, and she could get used to someone like him right now. Someone who understood, who would wrap her in a tender embrace and let her rest her head on his shoulder.

"I'd better be going. It's getting late."

"Sure. I understand."

She had a feeling he really did.

Downstairs, the girls let out long groans when she announced she was leaving.

"Do you have to go? Can't you stay for longer?" Georgie's pitiful face made her smile.

Livvy looked up at her with sad eyes and a pout. "You haven't had any ice cream yet. We always have ice cream on Sunday night."

Nina's heart was filled with gratitude knowing the girls weren't anxious for her to leave.

She gave each of the girls a kiss. "I'll come again. I promise."

"You'd better, young lady." Walt's stern tone was softened by the glint in his eyes.

The dogs trotted to her side, and she gave them each a pat, suddenly very reluctant to leave this sweet family.

Bret helped her into his SUV for the ride home, and she let the day's events replay in her mind. She'd thoroughly enjoyed the afternoon with Bret's family, but it had left her feeling adrift and buffeted by a rolling sea of emotions. Moments of contentment, mingled with swirls of melancholy seeing the girls play on the lawn, the lighthearted banter over the meal, the family atmosphere. But there'd been unexpected moments of deep sorrow and a sense of loss. It was a life she'd never have again, and she wanted it. More than she'd ever realized before.

"Are you okay? Did we wear you out?"

"No, not at all. It was a lovely afternoon. You have a delightful family."

She glanced sideways at Bret. Could she ever find it in her heart to love again? Her widows were struggling with the painful battle between hanging on to the old love and yet finding room and freedom to love again. No. First she had to find the flaw in herself that kept failing those she loved. Then maybe she could begin to think about loving again.

When she did, she hoped it would be with a man like Bret.

## Chapter Six

Bret stole a glance at his passenger. The afternoon had gone much better than he'd expected. Nina was staring out the windshield, head resting on the seatback. She seemed relaxed, but he wasn't sure. He couldn't tell if she'd had a good time today, or if she was regretting it. He had a feeling all the family time might have left her a little sad. Thankfully, the day had been so busy, he'd barely had time to think about his shocking discovery. But now, alone in the car, it rushed back at him full force.

Bret eased to a halt at the red light, resisting the urge to look at Nina again. He was beginning to understand what she'd been through. Losing her child and her husband so close together had been too much. He wanted to fix it for her, to bring back the warmth and joy that

Norm had described. He wanted to meet that woman. He doubted that would ever happen. Not when she learned the truth. He had to tell her, but how and when? He'd have to think this through before he did anything. Timing and opportunity would be crucial.

Maybe he could probe a bit and get an idea on her emotions about her husband. But there wasn't enough time on the short ride back to her apartment. He made a quick decision. "I was wondering if you could help me out with something."

"If I can."

"I have to choose a birthday gift for Georgie."

Nina chuckled softly. "Well, it had better be either a princess dress or a puppy. She mentioned it at least a dozen times today."

"Yeah. She reminds me every day."

"Which is it?"

"Puppy. Would you mind riding with me to help select the dog?"

"Are you bringing it home today?"

"No, just choosing the right one. I really want it to be a surprise."

"Shouldn't she pick it out herself?"

"If she were a normal kid, but no. She'd take one look at the five pups in the litter and demand them all. I'm willing to take on one more dog, but not that many."

"I see your point. I'd love to help. Who can resist a litter of warm puppies?"

"Thanks."

"It's the least I can do for that delicious meal. Your dad is quite the grill master. And a matchmaker."

"Sorry about that. He thinks I won't be happy until I'm married again. I can't make him see that I'm not cut out for marriage. If I was, it would have worked the first time. How about you? You think you'll ever marry again?"

"No. I'm not good at it either."

Bret studied her a moment. Strange. Norm always spoke of his marriage and his wife in such loving terms, Bret had assumed it was a happy one. His curiosity grew. He wanted to ask about her husband, but he sensed pushing too hard would get him nowhere. Maybe something general. "How long ago did you lose your husband?"

"Three years."

She'd kept her face to the car window when she replied. He decided to push a little more. "How did it happen?"

"It shouldn't have happened. He shouldn't have been there. He was supposed to be safe and protected." She clasped her purse a little closer in her lap. "So, how much farther are we going? This is very rural."

Nina was not going to talk about her husband. Just as well. He had a lot of soul-searching to do first.

"Not much farther. It's actually a straight shot from Main Street to the Central Highway."

If she was this reluctant to talk about her husband, how would he ever be able to tell her who he was and what had happened that day under the scorching Middle Eastern sun? The knot in his gut grew, but he ignored it. He couldn't dwell on what he'd discovered until he was alone. He couldn't let Nina see his distress. Not yet.

"Your daughters are adorable. They're nice young ladies, Bret. You should be proud."

"I am. Very."

"May I ask, what do they know about their mother? They seemed a bit vague about her leaving."

Bret set his jaw. It was a subject he didn't like to discuss. "We don't talk about her. Dad keeps telling me I should, but I don't really want them to know what she was like. How can I tell them she didn't love them enough to hang around?"

"I can understand that. But if you never talk about her, little minds will come up with reasons that put them at the center of things."

"What do you mean?"

"They might start to imagine that she left because of something they did or didn't do. That's a big burden for little ones to carry, don't you think?"

The old yellow farmhouse appeared from around the curve in the road ahead, and Bret exhaled a sigh of relief. Picking out the puppy would put an end to this subject and keep his mind occupied for a while longer.

Nina leaned forward in her seat. "Oh, how charming. I always thought it would be nice to live in an old farmhouse."

"Deb and Howard have done a lot of remodeling to the place. Deb runs a foster program for dogs. One of the many reasons Georgie loves to come here. Their little girl, Addie, is her best friend."

A tall, slender woman with bright red hair came toward them from the barn as they approached. Bret introduced her as Debra Randolph.

"I hope Addie isn't here."

Deb smiled and shook her head. "I knew better. If she was here, she'd blab to Georgie first thing tomorrow morning at school. She's at her grandma's. Let me show you the litter. The pups will be weaned in a few weeks, so you can take yours anytime after that. Does Georgie have a preference, male or female?'

Bret hunkered down beside the small pen where the five little dogs were playing. They all rushed to the edge to greet him. Nina stooped down beside him, uttering a soft sigh.

"They are so sweet. May I hold one?"

"Of course."

"My daughter has only one requirement. It has to have spots because she's decided its name is going to be Spotty."

"Well, then you'll probably want this little guy." Deb picked up a wiggly puppy and held it out to Bret. "He has a sweet temperament, and he has a spot on his tail, one on each ear and a couple down his back. Think that's enough?"

Bret held the pup close, scratching his neck gently. The little dog looked up at him with big black eyes. "I think she'll take to him at first sight. Will you hold him for us? I'll come by on her birthday and pick him up."

He glanced over at Nina, who had made friends with a furry little dog who had wandered up to her and was lavishing her with attention, causing her to giggle. The sound wound its way deep into his being. He wished he could make her happy all the time. His discovery surged back into his mind. That was out of the question. There was no way he could ever make her happy with the truth he carried.

"You have a new friend."

Nina smiled and stroked the dog again. "She's sweet, isn't she?"

Deb nodded. "She is. And she's housebroken and available for adoption. Would you like to take her home with you?"

"Oh, no. I'm not sure my apartment allows dogs. But she is a sweetheart."

Nina was quiet on the ride home, though she seemed to be in a calm, reflective mood. It might be a good time to tell her, but he didn't have the heart or the courage. He pulled up to her apartment and shut off the engine. "Thanks for going with me to pick out Georgie's dog."

"I enjoyed it. I enjoyed the whole day. Thank you for inviting me. I like your family. And your girls are very sweet."

"They were on their best behavior. You didn't get an accurate picture of the little divas. Sooner or later, they'll show their true colors."

Nina smiled. "You're exaggerating. I'm sure they are good kids."

"They are. Now, if I could do something with my dad."

"I'll see you in the morning." She smiled and got out of the car. Bret watched until she disappeared inside, and then he headed home, his spirits sinking with each mile.

He relived the moment when he'd seen the photo. He couldn't believe what he was seeing. How could his chaplain be Nina's husband? What were the chances? He'd prayed he was mistaken, but Nina had confirmed it. Alone, the impact of his discovery began to suffocate him, pressing in on his chest, making it hard to breathe.

Guilt and regret darkened his thoughts. It was all he could do to get home. In the driveway, he lowered his forehead against the steering wheel and tried to make sense of it all.

Norm Grant, the chaplain he'd vowed to protect with his life, was Nina's husband, Chip. *Lord, why are You doing this to me?* He carried enough guilt over Norm's death, but having to face the man's widow, a woman he was starting to care for, was too cruel to bear. How could he ever tell her the truth? The thought of seeing the horror and hate in her pretty eyes made him sick to his stomach.

The sound of tapping on the window forced him to lift his head. His father peered in at him, his face lined with concern. Bret opened the door and climbed out. He felt twenty years older than his dad at the moment.

"What's happened? Are you sick?"

Bret nodded, running a hand down his face. "We need to talk."

Walt cupped Bret's neck with his hand in a comforting gesture. "Let's go out back."

"Where are the girls?"

"Watching a movie. They really liked your lady friend. They're already asking when she'll be back. She's a keeper, that one."

Bret's heart sank. He agreed, but not for him. His family had already started to fall for Nina. What would happen when she learned the truth? He had a pretty good idea. She'd hate him and probably run back to Chicago on the next flight.

On the back deck, Bret sank into a chair, anxiously rubbing his chin. "Dad, I'm in a mess, and I don't know how to deal with it."

"What kind of mess?" Walt sat on the edge of his chair, leaning forward, listening intently. Bret drew comfort from the knowledge that his father would always be truthful and his wisdom had smoothed many a situation. "I saw a picture of Nina's husband today. He was Norm Grant."

It took his dad a moment to connect the dots. "As in, Chaplain Norm Grant?"

Bret watched the shock and horror play across his dad's face.

"Oh, my."

"I have no idea what to do."

"Why didn't you know this sooner?"

"She never talks about him. The few times I've asked about him, she'd become very defensive and withdrawn. She called him Chip. It's a family name or something. She goes by Johnson now, her maiden name."

"You never contacted the wife after his death?"

"I tried but could never catch her. I sent her a note but never heard back. I just assumed she didn't want to hear from me. I wouldn't if the situation were reversed. Why would she want to talk to the man who got her husband killed."

"That wasn't your fault."

"It was. I was the chaplain's assistance officer. He was my responsibility. What am I going to do?"

"You have to tell her. The sooner, the better."

"Dad, she's been through so much already. She lost her daughter and her husband, and now I'm supposed to tell her, 'Hey, I'm the guy who failed to save your husband. Want to come to my house for dinner?'"

"Do you want her to come back for dinner?"

"Dad." Bret stood and paced around, running a hand down the back of his neck. "It doesn't matter what I want. Once she learns the truth, she'll never speak to me again. I don't want to hurt her like that."

"So, you do like her. She's perfect for you, ya know. I could tell right away. And the girls think she's awesome."

He stared at his dad. Had the man lost his mind? He'd just dropped a huge emotional bomb on him, and he was still trying to play yenta. "I need your help here. What am I going to do?"

"Tell her. Then, when she's recovered from learning the truth, tell her in detail what happened that day. Moment by moment. Tell her what you know about her husband. She'll want to hear that."

"And torture her even more? No. I can't."

Walt came to his side, resting a hand on his shoulder. "You'll have to face this sooner or later. Sooner is always better. Waiting will only complicate things."

"Dad, she's so fragile. You should have seen her that day when she told me about losing her daughter. I was afraid if I said the wrong thing, she'd shatter like a piece of glass."

"I think you underestimate her. She's strong. She may not realize it herself yet, but she's tough."

"You don't know that. You've only met her a couple of times."

"I knew your mom was the woman for me after one date. Don't discount the Sinclair evaluation gene. Seriously, take some time to sort this out. Then take my advice and get this stuff out in the open."

Sleep that night was impossible. Each time he drifted off, his mind would replay the explosion, and he'd see Chaplain Norm darting ahead before he could stop him. When he woke, his whole body twisted with regret and guilt. Each time he pictured confessing to Nina who he was, he got a pounding headache that refused to succumb to aspirin. It was going to be a long day. He was actually glad he wasn't driving Nina to work this morning, even though the emptiness in the car closed around him like a heavy coat. He wasn't ready to face her yet, and he had no idea when he would be. There was never a good time or place—or the right words—for something like this.

He slipped quietly into his office, thankful that Nina hadn't spotted him as he came in. What a coward he was.

Dottie looked up and smiled as Nina entered the office Monday morning. "So, how was your first weekend in your own place? And how was the walk to work?"

"Wonderful. It's so nice to be settled again and out of that hotel. The walk over here was very peaceful and invigorating."

"Ha. You might change your mind when it's August and the temperature is ninety-eight, with ninety-eight percent humidity, first thing in the morning."

"I probably won't be here then. Kathryn will be back in July, remember?" A twinge of sadness zinged through her nerves. She hadn't expected that. She'd grown attached to her life here. "Thank you again for the furniture and for taking me to the grocery."

Dottie waved off the comment. "You'd have made ten trips to the store if you'd had to carry all that food. Filling a pantry for the first time is a big job. So, how was your cookout with the Sinclairs? And what did you think of old Walt?"

Nina cringed and shrugged. "I think he likes playing matchmaker."

"Oh, he doesn't play. He's a full-time, card-carrying, founding member of the club. No one escapes his schemes."

"You know him?"

"Oh, sure. We go to the same church. I've known his family for years." She shrugged. "I think he's gotten worse since Sylvia left. He's determined to find Bret a wife."

"I'm not sure Bret wants that. He's pretty sour on marriage. He told me how his wife dropped the kids on his dad and left while he was deployed."

Dottie stopped and frowned. "Is that what he told you?"

"Yes. He had to take an early discharge and come home."

"That part is true, but she didn't drop the girls off anywhere. She called Walt and told him to come get the girls, and she walked out. She left those babies all alone. Thank God Walt didn't live far. I hate to think of what could have happened in just a few minutes."

Nina's stomach flipped over. "I had no idea. No wonder he's so down on marriage."

"I can't understand a mother who would be so heartless and neglectful as to leave her little ones alone and unprotected for any reason."

Nina rested her hand near her throat. Like a mother who failed to protect her daughter by neglecting to activate the safety lock on her car door? Her mind fogged over with regret, and she had to struggle to pay attention to what Dottie was saying.

"Mr. Abbott called and said he'd be a few minutes late. Traffic accident on the highway slowed him down."

"Okay. I think I'll look over his file in the meantime."

"And there's going to be cake and goodies in the break room today. Anita just became a grandma, so we're celebrating."

Nina slipped into her office and sat at her desk, closing her eyes. Neglect. Bret's wife had deliberately risked her children's safety. Bret must have been frantic. She was glad Walt was there. She had a better understanding of his attitude now and his firm resistance to his father's matchmaking attempts. He would never trust another woman with his girls. They were his life. Seeing them together yesterday had made that abundantly clear. Her heart ached for him. He was a good man. Hardworking, devoted, kind and considerate. A good catch. Not that she was fishing.

So, what would he say if he learned about her own neglectful behavior? How she'd been so busy and preoccupied that she'd forgotten to double-check the lock on the car door, and Molly bolted from the back seat and into the path of an oncoming car.

Her walk to work this morning had been calming and peaceful, and it had buoyed her spirits. The exercise would do her body good, and the charming neighborhood with its old trees and lovely landscaped yards would bring her joy. But Dottie's revelation had shattered her good mood. She doubted if Bret would be so helpful and friendly once that fact came to light.

She liked Bret. A lot. He was the first man since Chip she'd been attracted to, but she better halt that right now. She was meant to be alone. She had to take comfort from the knowledge that she was enjoying her job again, that she had her own place and she'd even started her walk back to the Lord. That was enough. As far as Bret was concerned, she'd keep a safe distance. No more trips to pick out puppies. Strictly coworkers. It should be easy now that she wasn't relying on him for transportation.

She wasn't ready to admit that she relied on him for other things. Like friendship, gentle support and understanding.

If she were wise, she'd stop relying on those things, as well.

* * *

Dottie leaned in the doorway, midafternoon, pulling Nina's attention from the file she was studying. "It's time for the get-together. You coming?"

Her first impulse was to say no, but she had promised to turn over a new leaf, and that included attending the functions the other business owners held. "Sure."

Dottie smiled. "Good girl. You can't hide in here forever, you know." She took Nina's arm as they left the office and walked toward the break room.

Most of the owners were already there, and the cake was being served up. Nina greeted them and took the plate offered to her. "What are we celebrating today?"

Jackie, Bret's secretary, smiled. "Well, first off, Anita is a brand-new grandma." She raised her plastic cup as everyone applauded and shouted congratulations, and Anita held up a picture of the new baby. Nina had a vivid memory of the day Molly was born. She'd never known such intense pride and joy.

Jackie swung her attention in Nina's direction. "The other reason is because rumor has it that one of us just got a new home."

A few chuckles came from the others. She

handed Nina an envelope with a warm smile. "We wanted to help you get settled in your new place and welcome you to the building. We're all glad you're here."

Stunned, Nina could only blink and take the envelope. "This is so sweet of you. Thank you so much." Inside, she found a gift card to a local department store.

Someone stepped to her side.

"I told you they were a great bunch."

A thrill chased down her spine when she recognized Bret's slightly raspy voice. She looked up at him. His warm green eyes were gazing at her tenderly. "Yes, you did." She tried to look away, but it was impossible. They were connected, linked somehow, and she didn't want to end the moment. Her heart sped up, her palms grew damp and she scolded herself for her foolish attraction. She closed her eyes and shut out his gaze, and then she searched for a safe, neutral topic. "I've been thinking about some things you could do for your veterans' event that wouldn't be too complicated or expensive."

Bret grinned and shifted his weight as if he knew she was affected by his nearness. "That's great. Why don't you come to the office, and we'll discuss them?"

"I have a patient scheduled, but I can be there in an hour."

"Good. See you then." He winked and moved off to speak with Jeff and David, leaving her with an odd vibration inside, like a violin string that had been gently plucked.

So much for keeping her distance.

## Chapter Seven

Bret checked the clock again. Nina would be here any minute to discuss her ideas about the veterans' event. No big deal, except his palms were damp, his mouth was dry and beads of sweat were forming on his neck. He was behaving like a schoolkid with a crush. Or a man with a fascination he had no right to harbor. He'd stuffed the knowledge of Nina's husband into the dark recesses of his mind. He knew he'd have to face it sometime soon, but not yet. She'd been relaxed and friendly at the get-together today. That had to be a sign that she was growing more comfortable with her job and the people. He tried to forget the fact that she was only here for a few months. Then she'd be gone. The realization left a cold, hollow feeling inside his chest.

"Are you ready for me?"

Bret looked at her. He'd been ready for her to enter his life for a long time. "Yeah. Come on in. Alan will be joining us. I want him to hear your ideas."

He motioned her to a seat, caught by how the sunlight from the window made her auburn hair sparkle. Every day, she looked more and more like a local. She now dressed in light colors and cool fabrics, and she'd even started wearing strappy sandals in place of those ridiculous high heels. Unfortunately, that gave him fewer opportunities to rescue her from the deep-pile carpet. Thankfully, his partner entered and prevented him from voicing his thoughts.

Alan took the seat beside Nina and rubbed his hands together. "So, what have you got? I liked the bouncy-house idea—that'll draw a lot of kids. But what about the adults?"

Nina leaned forward. "An arts-and-crafts show would draw the grown-ups. Especially if you featured the vets and their wives or family members. I think visitors would really appreciate purchasing handmade things by the veterans. And your friend Deb could bring some dogs for adoption. Especially puppies. Kids will flock to see and hold puppies."

"That's a great idea. I'll call her this afternoon." Bret tapped a reminder into his computer.

Alan leaned forward in his chair, a big smile on his face. "This lady is amazing. You know, I was thinking that, with the park situated by the river, maybe we could set up a place for kids to fish."

"They'd love that." Bret nodded and made another notation. "I know just the guy to put it together. I'll call him."

"What about a bike parade for kids?" Nina glanced between the two men. "They could decorate them and ride through the park, and you could give small trophies for each age bracket."

Bret grinned. "I like it. And music. What about a band? I know a couple of vets who have a bluegrass group."

"Right." Alan snapped his fingers. "And I know a guy who has a gospel group."

"Do you think the chamber committee will go for these ideas?"

"I think so." Bret leaned back in his chair. "Especially if we can keep costs down. This is going to require a lot of volunteers."

Alan waved off the concern. "I think everyone will be willing to help since it's geared to bringing attention to the veterans, and hopefully that will translate into more attention on Phase II. I wish I could get the word out more. But marketing takes money, and we don't have that much to spare."

"Have you invited the media?" Nina glanced at Bret.

Bret nodded. "The chamber has, but last year the piece they filmed aired only a few times, which didn't do much good. We're hoping they'll air it again this year, and maybe when people see the announcement, they'll remember and come check it out."

Alan rubbed his temple. "What we need is something really different. Unusual. Something that will compel people to leave their TVs for the day."

Nina fell silent. Bret turned his gaze on her. She looked like she wanted to say something but was holding back. "Nina? You have another idea?"

She glanced at Alan before answering. "I do, but I don't want it to offend anyone, and it might be too personal, or even in bad taste."

Alan gave Nina his full attention. "I'm intrigued. Go on."

Nina bit her lip, clearly reluctant to speak.

"Do you remember the first day I met Alan? I was surprised by his prosthetic leg."

Alan chuckled. "That's nothing new. People are always curious about it."

"I know. I certainly was. I had a flood of questions pop into my head. But to ask would have been rude and maybe callous. So I kept silent. I didn't want to offend you or stare like you were some sideshow."

"No problem. It's natural. You get over that pretty quickly."

"What does this have to do with your idea?" Bret asked.

"Would it be possible to have a place where people could ask questions about prosthetics, a safe place where they could see artificial arms and legs, learn how they work, ask the vets how they lost their limbs and how hard it was to get used to the new devices?"

Bret met Alan's gaze. He could see the wheels turning.

Nina sighed. "I'm sorry. That was a bad idea. Totally inappropriate."

"No, not at all. It's a good idea. It just needs a bit of fine-tuning." Alan stood and paced the floor. "You know little kids are always staring at my leg when I wear shorts. I see their moms shushing them, not wanting to appear rude. It might be a good idea to let them see and touch and ask in a way that won't be awkward for either the vet or the guests."

Bret typed something into his computer. "We could also have some of the special equipment brought in on display for people to see, like a range of different legs and arms, the hand cycles and other specially designed sports items."

"Will it be hard to find vets to agree to participate?" Nina asked.

"No. Most people are familiar with the prosthetics thanks to TV shows and *Dancing with the Stars* and programs like that. But seeing it up close is different." Alan raised his hand for a high five. Nina complied with a giggle.

Bret's pulse skipped at the sound. "That's a great idea, Nina. I'll get right on it."

She sighed and leaned back in her chair. "I'm glad you weren't offended, Alan."

Bret chuckled. "The only thing that offends him is when a pretty girl doesn't fall for his lame pickup lines."

Nina took the steps to the old Foursquare slowly, admiring the flower pots she'd picked up yesterday to brighten up the front porch. Her half of it, anyway. Her little home was growing cozier by the day, and she loved the walk from the office, which gave her time to unwind and sort through her day. By the time she arrived at her apartment, she was ready to get comfy, have a bite to eat and relax.

Once inside the wide entrance, she inserted her key into the lock and turned it. The sound of the tumblers were unusually loud this evening. She glanced over her shoulder, and her gaze traveled down the long, shadowed hallway. Signs of construction still littered the space. The large home suddenly felt alarmingly empty, and she was struck by how alone she was here.

Quickly slipping inside her apartment, she locked the door behind her and shook off the uneasy sensation. After a quick meal, she curled up with a book on the sofa, but after reading the same paragraph three times, she gave up.

Something wasn't right. For the last three years, she'd relished her solitude. She deliberately distanced herself from friends and activities. Being alone was the only time she felt safe and strong. Like some nocturnal animal, she'd scurry into her hidey-hole, lock the door and stay buried until morning, when she was forced to emerge and go about her job.

Only tonight the solitude didn't comfort or soothe her. Instead she felt antsy, dissatisfied. The feeling had been building since the cookout at Bret's. There had been moments at his house when her whole body ached as she watched the girls play, remembering her own happy times with Molly. Yet there'd been little moments when she'd felt a sense of belonging.

Was it possible she missed her old social life? She hadn't always been a hermit. She and Chip had often entertained friends. Molly had a girlfriend at the house most weekends, and Nina had been active in her church and her community. That had all ended when Molly died, and after Chip left, she'd withdrawn even more.

Surprisingly, she'd enjoyed the building get-together the other day, and she'd been enthused by sharing her ideas for the veterans' event with Bret and Alan. Maybe it was time to stop avoiding life and start participating again. She missed having friends, going to lunch, looking forward to weekend activities. Being involved in her own life.

All she had to do was find the courage to act on this new revelation. Easier said than done. Understanding a specific behavior was one thing. Acting upon it was something else entirely.

Nina kept her expression neutral, her breathing even, but it was growing harder to control her frustration and her anxiety. Longtime patient Richard Fontana had requested a special session, but he'd taken exception to her suggestion that perhaps he should take a step back and examine his behavior from a different angle. Sadly, she'd misjudged the man's progress, and instead of begrudgingly agreeing as Kathryn's file indicated was his usual response, he'd grown red in the face and glared. He started a long diatribe about her inferior abilities and Kathryn's superior ones, and she'd been unable to interrupt him.

"Mr. Fontana. I meant no disrespect. Therapy is a slow and sometimes painful journey, and taking a step back and reexamining our internal motives can be beneficial."

"You have no idea what my motives are. They go beyond that file folder of yours. Dr. Harvey understood. She would never suggest that there was something deeply wrong with me. I don't know where you got your diploma, but it obviously was from up in one of those unfeeling Yankee colleges."

Fontana pivoted and marched to the door. "I don't think we have anything else to say to one another." He strode across the reception area, and then spun on his heel and glared at Dottie. "Do not schedule any further appointments for me with this quack. I'll wait until Doc Harvey gets back, or else I'll find a more competent therapist." He sent a fierce glare in Nina's direction. "And you might want to put a sign on the door that says Enter at Your Own Risk."

Nina sighed and leaned against the door frame of her office. Her knees were shaking, and her hands were damp. She'd never handled confrontations well. Thankfully, she'd only had a few of her previous patients get upset with her. Mostly they would rant about the people in their lives. Mr. Fontana was a first.

Dottie came around the desk and stopped at her side. "What clamped an alligator to his tail?"

"I suggested he might take some time to look inside himself for answers to his problems, but he didn't like that idea."

"I heard."

Nina tilted her head back with a heavy sigh. "Oh, Dottie, what should I do? I've lost Kathryn a patient. I'm supposed to be filling in and keeping her people on course, not upsetting their emotional balance."

"Don't worry about him. He's probably just uneasy about talking to someone new. It's easier to lash out than try something different. You know that. Kitty knew this might happen with a couple of people."

"What if he doesn't come back? What if he finds a new therapist? At this rate, Kathryn won't have a practice to come back to."

"Nonsense. You're doing a great job. Don't let one insecure, self-absorbed middle-aged man get to you."

Nina stifled a grin. "He is self-absorbed, isn't he?"

Dottie rolled her eyes. "Ya think?"

"I want to do a good job for Kathryn. I want to be responsible. Not leave her a bunch of patients who've lost the ground they'd gained."

"You won't. The Widow's Walk ladies love you, and the session with Mrs. Warrick and her daughter went really well yesterday. She made a point to tell me on her way out."

"It did, didn't it. I really want to help them."

"You will." Dottie went back to the desk. "This might make you feel better." She handed Nina a slip of paper with a name and phone number.

"What's this?"

"A potential new patient. She's an acquaintance of one of the widows, and she would like to start therapy, but she wants to talk with you first." Dottie smiled. "Your first official patient."

Nina smiled. "Is it okay to take her on? I mean, Kathryn won't mind?"

"Didn't she say in her letter that you're free to do that? Go for it. Besides, you might decide to stay here in Hastings and start your own practice. Maybe you and Kitty could be partners."

"That's a nice idea, but no. I can't stay here. I'd never fit in. I'm a big-city girl."

"Who's a big-city girl?"

The women turned to face Bret, who had stepped into the office.

"I am."

"Are you leaving? So soon? You've only been here a few weeks. Is Kitty coming back early?"

Dottie held up her hand. "Slow down, big fella. Nobody is going anywhere. Everything is just peachy."

"Except I might have lost Kathryn a patient this morning."

"Don't listen to her." Dottie dismissed his concern.

"What happened?"

Nina quickly explained.

Bret stepped closer, lightly touching her arm. "He didn't hurt you, did he?"

Nina tried to ignore the electric charge skipping along her nerve endings. "Only my ego and self-confidence. Maybe I'm not cut out for this job after all. I've been away too long. I just wanted to keep her patients on track."

"I don't know much about Kitty's practice, but I do know people, and I know there's no such thing as a straight track. Lives twist and turn, curl back on themselves and take off in new directions without warning. In the end, it all seems to work out. People come up against a fear, and they run away instead of facing it."

The level of understanding in his tone touched her. "You're pretty wise for a soldier."

"Not really. Just lessons learned from life the hard way."

Nina wanted to ask him about those lessons. She knew the story of his failed marriage, but what other heartbreaks had he known?

The question was still circling in the back of her mind when she closed up that evening. She met Bret coming out of his office as she stepped into the hall.

"Things go better this afternoon, I hope?"

"Yes, thank goodness."

Bret closed the distance between them, his green eyes lit with a friendly light. "I was wondering if you'd like to grab a bite to eat. There's a little place right around the corner we can go to. I want to tell you about the chamber meeting last night. They have some concerns about our ideas."

"All right. I'm anxious to hear what they said." Nina stilled the small voice in her head that reminded her she could just as easily talk to Bret right here in the hallway. But the idea of spending time with Bret was too tempting to resist. Her common sense said to stay away from the handsome veteran, but her heart was urging her to spend time with him.

She was setting herself up for a big heartbreak, but the journey there was going to be very pleasant.

Settled in a quiet corner of a nearby café, Bret organized his thoughts. He'd told Nina he wanted to tell her about the chamber meeting, but he'd had other motives, as well. She'd been in good spirits, and he hoped this might be the right time to tell her who he was. He doubted she would cause a scene in a public place. Then once she'd calmed down, he'd tell her the whole story and pray that she could someday forgive him.

Nina took a sip of her sweet tea. "What were the chamber's concerns?"

"Their biggest objection was about letting people ask questions about the prosthetics. They liked the idea but are worried that it might stir up controversy among some people."

"Does that mean the idea is rejected?"

Bret shook his head. "They suggested we cut it to one or two very short, controlled sessions and see how it goes. Alan and I are working out the details. He's asked a friend of his, Leslie Delmont, another vet, to help out."

"But they were okay with our other ideas? The fishing and the bike parade?"

"Those got the green light. I've already mentioned it to my girls. Olivia is looking forward to the fishing, and Georgie is already designing the decorations for her bike."

Nina smiled, and her blue eyes held a sparkle. "I really do enjoy your girls. They are so much fun."

Her comment caught him off guard and opened the way to another subject he wanted to discuss. "If you really mean that, I could use a babysitter for a few hours this Saturday. Dad is working with the Home for Soldiers project all day, and the regular sitter will be out of town. Alan and I have a meeting with some vets about our services. I don't suppose you'd be interested in watching the girls for a while? I'll understand if you're tied up, or if you'd rather not, that's okay, too."

"I'd love to watch the girls. What time should I be there?"

Bret reached over and took her hand. "Thanks. I know the girls will be thrilled."

The contact between them vibrated. Bret told himself to release her hand, to keep his distance, but he couldn't let go. The warmth in her blue eyes fueled his hope that she might have feelings for him. Then the ugly truth of his failure rose in the back of his mind. He slowly slipped his hand away. Maybe now was the time. He searched for the words, but none came.

"Nina, we need to talk. I have something to tell you that might be difficult to hear."

Her smile faded into a frown, but before she could comment, her cell rang. She glanced at the screen, and then she pushed back from her chair.

"I have to take this. I'll be right back."

She hurried off, and he watched as she paced in a small circle and nodded. He guessed she was trying to calm someone down. When she returned to the table, he could see she was concerned. "Everything okay?"

"No. One of my patients is having a crisis. He's going to meet me back at the office. I'm sorry. I wanted to relax and enjoy our meal."

"That's okay. Go. We'll talk later. Do you need me to do something?"

"No. I can handle it. But thanks. I appreciate that you're there for me."

"Call me if you need a ride home after dark."

She smiled and nodded before leaving. Bret watched her leave, his heart heavy with regret. He had to get the truth off his conscience before he went crazy, but the right time never seemed to materialize. His dad was right—the longer he put it off, the harder and more complicated it became. It wasn't a matter of simply coming clean anymore. His heart was entangled with the lovely therapist, and telling her would not only break her heart, but seriously damage his own.

Doubt slammed into Nina the moment Bret walked out of the house Saturday afternoon. She'd promised to watch the girls while Bret attended a meeting. She'd even looked forward to spending time with Olivia and Georgie. The girls had greeted her with squeals of excitement and hugs, but now, standing in the middle of their family room, her old fears spiraled up inside.

These two little girls were under her care. The sense of responsibility pressed in. What if something happened? What if she made another mistake and one of them got hurt?

She rubbed her temple to ease the throbbing. Why had she agreed to this? What had she been thinking? She hadn't been able to take care of her own child, so how could she take care of Bret's girls, even for a short time?

Georgie tugged on her hand. "Come on, Miss Nina. We want to color."

"No. I have a sticker book I want her to play with." Olivia held up the book with princesses on the front.

Nina allowed herself to be steered to the breakfast room table with a view of the backyard. It was raining, and she was suddenly grateful for the inclement weather. She could keep the girls inside playing games and dolls and coloring. Outside offered too many opportunities for falls and injuries.

Yes. Rain was a blessing today. She sat down and gazed at the two sweet eager faces across the table. Her worries washed away like the rain on the roof. For two hours, she'd get to spend time with these adorable girls. It had been a long time since she'd played with coloring books and dolls. It sounded like fun.

An hour later, Nina looked around the breakfast room at the cluttered mess of books, crayons and various other toys.

Olivia walked into the room with a large box, a doll-sized Jeep and a bag. "Now we can play Barbies."

Georgie hopped up on a chair. "I want to play."

"No. You never do it right."

"I do too."

"Before we do that, we need to clean up and put these books and things away."

"We're good cleaner-uppers. Daddy says it's important to pick up our messes. And we make lots of messes."

Livvy giggled. "Gramps says we're the worst he's ever seen."

Nina laughed out loud. "I think he may be right."

Olivia looked at her with a mischievous expression. "Maybe we should wait until we're done with the Barbies before we clean up. We're just going to make another big mess. Then we can do it all at once."

Nina recognized the ploy. Livvy didn't want to stop playing to take time to clean up. She couldn't blame her. "I suppose that would be okay."

Livvy squealed and settled in the sunroom to play with the dolls, unpacking an amazing amount of doll furniture, clothes and other accessories. Nina finished putting the ball gown on the Barbie doll and handed it to Livvy, watching as she tucked her in the pink Jeep, getting her ready for the princess ball she was attending. Georgie was busy brushing her doll's hair. The girls were so content, so sweet, just watching them filled her with a powerful nurturing feeling. She'd loved being Molly's mother, loved taking care of her, watching her, playing with her. Her death had left a huge void in that department. Yet now, with Bret's girls, those feelings were being reborn.

What would it be like to raise these girls? To see them every day, watch them learn and grow? How sweet would it be to tuck them in at night, to hold them close each morning? Fanciful thought. That would never happen. Bret had experienced the neglect of one woman in his life. He'd never allow someone like her into his life again.

But she could enjoy the moments when they came. When she left Hastings, she'd have lovely memories to take with her. Memories of what might have been.

Bret shook raindrops off his umbrella, and then set it in the stand in the mudroom to dry. Peals of laughter, mingled with giggles, assaulted his ears. He stopped, smiling at the sound. His girls giggled a lot, but it was the richer, musical laugh of a woman that was rising above the girlish squeals. Apparently, his concerns about leaving Georgie and Olivia with Nina were unfounded.

He stepped to the archway leading into the

breakfast room and peeked in. The kitchen table was littered with coloring books, crayons and various games. In the sunroom beyond, he saw Nina seated in a wicker chair and Georgie leaning against her leg, holding up a doll for Nina to see. Livvy was on her knees, moving her two dolls around on the ottoman. She looked up and said something to Nina, who smiled and nodded.

A sharp shaft of longing pierced his chest. This was what he wanted in his life. A complete family, a woman to come home to, and a mother for his girls. Nina belonged here. She fit in as if made for his family. But he knew there was no way it could work out.

"Daddy!"

Georgie raced toward him, her arms high, a happy smile on her face. He scooped her up and held her close, her little arms squeezing his neck. "Did you and Miss Nina have fun?"

His daughter nodded enthusiastically. "We colored and played games and Livvy let me play with her bestest sticker book. I had a page just for me."

Olivia came and gave him a hug. "Can Miss Nina babysit us all the time?"

Bret laughed. If only. "You'll have to ask her about that." He carried Georgie into the sunroom, his heart skipping wildly in his chest. Every time he saw Nina, she became more beautiful. But he had to halt his growing attraction. "You survived, I take it."

"I did. We had a good time together."

Georgie whispered in his ear.

"She's a really good mommy. Can we keep her?"

Blood drained from his face. Why had she asked that question now? He'd already been blindsided with a call from their mother. His momentary delight in seeing his girls happy crashed.

He needed to think. What he really wanted was to talk to Nina and get her advice, but he couldn't.

"Hey, guys. Did you miss me?"

Walt entered the kitchen with his usual bravado, and for once, Bret didn't mind. He welcomed the distraction.

His father gave Nina a quick hug. "Why don't you stay and have supper with us? We're having pork chops tonight."

Bret met Nina's gaze and was surprised to see concern in the blue depths. A small frown creased her forehead. Had she realized he was troubled? Did she know him that well already?

"Thank you, Walt, but I need to go home. Bret, would you mind giving me a ride?"

Bless her heart, she was giving him a

chance to open up to her. "I'm ready when you are."

He waited as she said goodbye to the girls and obtained a promise from them that they would clean up all the toys.

Inside his SUV, he reached for the start button, but Nina took hold of his forearm, the warmth of her touch soothing some of his anxiety.

"What happened? I've never seen you this upset."

Bret held her gaze. "I thought I was hiding it pretty well."

"My therapist instinct is trained to see these things. Didn't your meeting go well?"

Another area of his life that had taken a nosedive today. "The meeting was fine, but the notification date for contracts from the government has passed, and we haven't heard anything."

"I'm so sorry. I know how much you've been counting on that." Nina squeezed his arm. "There's something else, isn't there?"

Bret held her gaze. How could she read him so well in such a short time? Was it merely her therapist training, or was it something more? Whichever it was, at this moment, he was grateful. "I got a call from Sylvia. She wants to see the girls." Nina's soft gasp told him she was as surprised as he'd been.

"Why now, after all this time? Is she allowed to see them?"

"I don't know. Maybe she's having belated maternal emotions." He set his jaw. "She has no rights or privileges at all. I have full custody, and it's up to me if I let her see the kids or not. She signed away all her rights, and didn't even ask for alimony. She just wanted out."

"What are you going to do?"

"I don't know. I've been thinking about what you said—how the girls might blame themselves for their mother's leaving. Do you think letting Sylvia see them is a good idea or not?"

"I can't answer that. On one hand, it would give them a chance to see her again and have a memory. On the other hand, it could confuse them. Only you know how your children might react." Nina leaned forward to look him directly in the eyes. "There's something else, isn't there?"

He looked into her compassionate blue eyes. He wanted to tell her who he was, clear the air and try to salvage their relationship. His whole world was twisting around him and growing more and more complicated. He also knew she'd know that awful sensation again, once he told her the truth. If only he could ignore the whole thing and pretend it never happened.

He started the engine. "Thanks for listening. I'd better get you home. I need to figure out what I'm going to do about Sylvia."

"Call if you need to talk more. Anytime. And let me know what you decide about the girls' mother."

Talking with Nina usually helped, but with the truth weighing on his shoulders, he didn't feel much better. Of all his problems right now, that one cut the deepest.

But he had two more pressing issues to resolve—Sylvia and the government contract. What was he going to do if they didn't get the contract? They'd have to cut back on their services, maybe lay off a couple of people.

First thing was to decide about Sylvia. He knew what he wanted to do, but he'd run it by his dad first. He didn't trust his own judgment right now. His cell phone rang as he pulled into his driveway. "Hey, Alan. What's up?"

"A little good news, I hope. Dad just talked to a guy he knows, and he says our contract application was still in the running." Alan's father was a congressman in Washington, DC, and had been keeping tabs on the contract situation.

*Thank You, Lord, for a ray of hope.* "Did he have any idea when the decision will be made?"

"Not for a few weeks yet."

"Then I guess we put all our efforts into the veterans' event and pray we can stir up some interest."

"I think it will. Have a little faith, buddy."

He had buckets of faith that he was in the right business, but he didn't have much when it came to working with the government. A soft ding brought a light to his phone screen, revealing an email from Kitty. He swiped the screen with his thumb and scanned the message. She wanted to know how Nina was doing. She would email her friend, too, but she wanted to hear from him before she did.

Bret leaned his head back in the seat. What should he tell her? *She's doing a great job, coming alive again, everyone likes her, my kids and my dad adore her, and I'm falling in love with her. There's only one problem.*

*I made her a widow.*

He couldn't think about that now. He had to decide what to do about Sylvia, and he had a veterans' event to finalize. That meant putting telling Nina the truth on hold. After that, he wouldn't let anything stand in his way. Not even the lovely woman who visited his dreams every night.

# Chapter Eight

Nina's good spirits carried her the next few days. She was starting to feel like her old self, and she liked the feeling. She walked out of her office Thursday, thinking how strange it was to see Dottie at her desk. She'd switched her work days due to a doctor's appointment.

Dottie motioned her to her desk, smiling in delight. "You have two new patients. One is a single mom who just moved to town, and she's looking for a good therapist. She's a widow, as well, and is in need of some help during her move here. The other is a mother and son who need help learning how to communicate before their relationship deteriorates any further. I've scheduled them both for next Thursday."

"Did you tell them I'm a substitute?"

"I did. They weren't concerned."

Nina bit her lip. She hadn't anticipated

growing her friend's practice. But she was starting to gain patients of her own, and it was a scary thought. Kathryn had files and notes on all the people she'd counseled, which had given Nina a clear understanding of each one before she met with them. But these new ones were coming to her like blank pages. She'd have to evaluate, analyze and determine their treatment on her own.

A surge of confidence swelled inside. Maybe when she went back home, instead of looking for a new job, she could start her practice again. It would take a while to get it up and running, but it might be worth it. In the midst of her losses, she'd forgotten how much satisfaction she derived from helping others.

"Kitty will be so proud of you."

"Are you sure she won't be upset? I don't want her to think I'm taking over her practice."

"Nonsense. She was hoping your time here would help you get out of your rut and start living again." Dottie's hand flew to her mouth, eyes filled with regret. "Oh, I'm sorry. I wasn't supposed to tell you that."

"Did she really think I was in a rut?"

Dottie pursed her lips. "Well, weren't you?"

The truth stung. But she couldn't deny it. She hadn't thought of it as a rut, but she had sensed on some level that she needed to get up and move again. She'd been stagnant too long. "I suppose."

"And look at all you've accomplished since coming down here with us. You're more relaxed, you've made friends, you have a nice young man to spend time with and you're keeping Kitty's practice running and growing."

"Oh, well, some of that might be true, but the part about the young man isn't. There is nothing going on between me and Bret."

"Why not? He's a great catch."

"I'm sure he is, and he's a nice man, but I'm not looking for any kind of relationship."

"Maybe it's looking for you?"

Nina arched her brows. "Then I'll keep the door shut."

Dottie chuckled. "You can try, but when love comes knocking, it won't walk away so easily. You'll see. In fact, I'd be willing to predict—"

The office door suddenly whooshed open, and a large man entered, his angry gaze scanning the two women. "Which one of you is the doctor here?"

Nina faced him, keeping her expression calm and pleasant. "I'm Ms. Johnson, the therapist. Dr. Harvey is out of the country. Can I help you?"

The man's expression turned dark and threatening. "What right do you have to tell my wife to divorce me? Who do you think you are, messing in people's lives?"

Nina stood her ground, even as her knees wobbled and her anxiety spiked. "Who is your wife?"

"Helen Crosby."

Nina quickly made a mental search for the woman's history. A drunken husband who verbally abused her and tried to control her every move. The woman wanted to break away, but had lacked the courage. It was why she'd started coming to see Kathryn.

"I never told your wife to file for divorce."

He took a threatening step forward and loomed over her. "Then why did she go to an attorney? Tell me that."

"You'll have to ask her."

"No. You're the one. I agreed to let her talk to the shrink lady, but then you come along and all of a sudden she's calling lawyers and thinking she can walk out on me. That's on you, lady."

He pointed a finger so close to her face, she could smell his sweat. Her heart pounded.

Dottie came from behind her desk and stood

at Nina's side. "Mr. Crosby, I think you'd better leave before I call security."

Nina appreciated the bluff, but she knew there was no full-time security in the building.

Crosby took another step forward, causing Nina to step back and bump into a chair. She steadied herself and tried to remain calm and firm, despite the fear clogging her throat. "If you'll calm down, we can discuss this, I'm sure."

"No. You and that shrink lady have been messing with her head long enough. What's her problem, anyhow? She's been coming here for over a year, and I haven't seen any difference. So what's her big hang-up?"

"I'm sorry, but I can't discuss my patient's issues with you. That's a private matter between your wife and her therapists."

"I'm her husband!"

His shout hurt her ears.

"And I'm the man who is going to escort you from the building unless you calm down and back away from Ms. Johnson."

The cold, threatening tone of Bret's voice was the most beautiful sound she'd ever heard. Relief washed through her body, and she grasped the chair arm for support when her knees nearly buckled. Crosby stepped aside, and Nina saw Bret filling the doorway with his broad shoulders and muscular body. Behind him, Alan stood ready to back him up, and a third man stood to Alan's side.

The cavalry had arrived.

"I'm talking to the shrink, so nose out, fella."

"And I'm telling you that you'd better leave. Or the deputy will haul you off to jail right now."

"What deputy? I don't see any cops. And I'm not breaking any laws. I just want some answers."

Nina watched as the third man raised a badge into the air, a satisfied smirk on his face. She had no idea why he was here, but guessed he was one of Bret's vets who was now a deputy.

Crosby huffed and puffed, but when Bret entered the room, and Alan stood at the door, he had a clear view of the uniformed officer.

He grumbled under his breath and tossed a glare at Nina. "We're not done with this."

Bret yanked Crosby's arm behind his back and shoved him toward the door. Alan took the other arm, and he and the deputy escorted the man out.

Bret came straight to her and pulled her into his arms. "Are you all right? He didn't hurt you, did he?"

She'd never felt so safe. His heart was beating rapidly under her ear, his arms were warm and secure, and she had no desire whatsoever to leave them. She'd fought a lot of battles over the last five years, all alone, without any help, and she'd survived. But the comfort she found in Bret's embrace was like a peaceful oasis, a safe place to go where someone else could do the fighting.

"No. He just scared me, that's all. How did you know he was here?"

"The shouting was the first clue. But Dottie gave us the heads-up."

"You called him? I didn't see you."

"I sure did. I wasn't going to let that bully come after you like that."

Bret laid his hand on the side of her face, gently brushing away a few strands of hair. "Alan and I came right over."

"And the deputy?"

"One of my vets who happened to be in the office, volunteering for the event. The Lord had it all under control."

"I guess He did."

"Are you sure you're okay?"

"I'm fine. Now." She looked up into his green eyes and saw them dilate. The affection she saw sent her heart beating erratically, and her knees weakened. A smile crept across her lips as she lowered her lashes. She hadn't behaved this way since she was a teenager and every glimpse of her crush made her smile like a silly goose. Bret must think she was an idiot.

She stole a glance at Bret and saw the same infatuated smile on his face. If Dottie hadn't been in the room, she would have giggled out loud. Instead she laid her hand on his chest and held his gaze. "Thank you again for coming to help."

"My pleasure. Anytime you need me, just send up a flare."

Bret turned and left the office, and Nina became aware of Dottie, who was staring at her with an amused smirk.

"So, there's nothing between you and the handsome soldier, huh? Right."

There was no denying it now.

Nina squinted at the rising sun as it pushed up over the trees in Riverside Park. They'd been blessed with perfect weather for Hastings' Military Appreciation Day. She'd prayed for sunny skies, and the Lord had heard her plea. White tented canopies of varying sizes were going up all over the park as the various groups set up their displays and attractions. The hum of generators filled the air as the two giant bouncy houses were being inflated. She was anxious to see them in action. Livvy and Georgie had talked of nothing else for days. They'd also pulled a promise from their dad to take them to the fishing hole set up along the banks of the Black River, which bordered the west side of the park.

Her job today was to act as go-for. Bret and Alan would be manning the Phase II tent, passing out flyers and pamphlets, answering questions and signing up new customers. Several Phase II employees and volunteers would back them up. Beside the main tent, Bret had created an enclosed area. The chamber had agreed to a short discussion on prosthetics, but it had to be private with a limited number of participants. They had also requested that people sign up ahead of time and be issued a ticket. Bret wasn't happy about the restrictions, but Alan had rolled with it and had been glad they had a starting point. He was convinced that next year's event would be bigger and better. Alan had decided to wear shorts so people could see his leg and ask questions. Another wounded soldier, Leslie Delmont, who had a prosthetic forearm, would be the other person in the Q&A sessions.

Bret placed a box on the folding table and

smiled. "Give me a hand, will you? We need to get these brochures out early."

Nina opened the slick trifold advertising pamphlet. "They turned out great. These should grab people's attention."

Nina filled the holders and spread some on the table near the other flyers and booklets on display. Bret stored the extras under the table, which had been covered with a red, white and blue plastic tablecloth.

"Thanks for helping today. You sure you don't mind being our runner today?"

"Not at all. But I wish I'd dressed a little cooler." She glanced down at her linen slacks and sleeveless shirt. "I don't own a pair of shorts, but I think I will soon."

"Smart girl."

"When are the girls coming?"

"Right after it opens. Dad is volunteering at the Home for Soldiers booth since he works with them. His shift is later in the morning. He's going to take them around, let them see things, then bring them over to me. Would you mind keeping an eye on them for a while later? I'll slip away as soon as I can and take them to the babysitter."

"I don't mind watching them. I've had a little experience with them."

Bret smiled warmly. "So you have. The girls

are still talking about the Barbie-doll ball. I think I'll call on you for help more often."

"I really like your girls. Georgie is a lot like Molly. So full of life and mischief. And Livvy reminds me of myself. I was a shy, wary kid growing up. I think that's why I became a psychologist. I was always trying to figure people out. Why did they do the things they did? Why did they choose the wrong path when the right one was so easy to follow?"

"Human nature. There's no accounting for that element."

Something in his eyes darkened, and she grew curious. There was so much she wanted to know about him. She'd been tempted to ask his father. She knew Walt would be more than happy to fill in all the blanks, but Bret would be mortified. Besides, she'd rather have him tell her of his own accord.

However, she knew something was bothering him. Had been for some time, and she couldn't figure it out. One moment he'd be warm and tender, and she had the feeling he was attracted to her the way she was to him, but then he'd suddenly pull away and throw up a shield. It was very strange. Of course he had warned her from the start that he wasn't looking for a relationship. His wife's abandonment had left deep wounds. She understood that since she had her own wounds to protect.

"Daddy!"

The event had been open to the public for nearly an hour when Nina looked up from the table where she was handing out tickets to the Q&A session and saw Olivia and Georgie racing across the grass toward their dad. Walt was following behind, pulling an ornately decorated two-wheel bike with training wheels. Georgie's entry into the bike parade. Olivia had declared she was too old for such baby stuff.

"There's my little sugarplums." Bret knelt down and caught a girl in each arm and applied a firm hug.

Nina's heart softened. Bret was such a big, strong man and yet he could turn to warm mush when it came to his daughters. Chip had been that way, too. Molly had him wrapped around her little finger. She waved at Walt, and then she focused on the couple who had approached the table.

"Hi, Miss Nina." Georgie smiled up at her from the other side of the table. "Grampy is going to take us fishing, and then to the bike parade. Do you think I'll win?"

Nina glanced at the bike now parked beside the Phase II table, its crepe-paper streamers and the purple feathers floating in the breeze. "I think you have a good shot at it. It's the most colorful bike I've seen so far."

"Will you come watch me in the parade?"

"I will. It comes right past our table, so I'll get a good look. Be sure and wave at me."

"I will." She waved and dashed off.

Olivia strolled up. A slight quirk to her mouth. "Do you really think she'll win?"

"I don't know, but I hope so. It would make her very happy."

Livvy nodded. "Yeah. She worked real hard on her bike. I helped her with the feathers and the beads."

"That was very sweet of you. You're a good big sister."

The child shrugged. "She's okay for a twerp, I guess."

The next hour passed in a blur. She'd helped replenish brochures and handouts. The crowds were growing, and the participants were all excited. Bret and Alan were beaming. Before she knew it, the announcement came that the bike parade was starting. She could see the starting line from her table. Bret came over to watch with her.

Marching music blared from the park speakers as bikes of all sizes and kids up to age twelve rolled past. Some participants threw candy to the crowd as they passed; others tossed beads. Bret explained it was a Southern thing that had started with tossing beads and trinkets from the Mardi Gras floats.

Georgie was in the middle of the pack, and her little legs pumped the pedals furiously as she rode, grinning from ear to ear, waving frantically as she passed. Nina's eyes stung. The child was so adorable. Bret whistled and shouted, the smile on his face and the light in his eyes telling of his pride for his littlest girl.

When the winners were announced a while later, Georgie received a second place for her age group. She proudly held up the ribbon and the small plastic trophy.

"I won!"

"Yes, you did." Bret gave her a big hug.

Livvy started to correct her, but a loud clearing of his throat and a shake of his head forestalled her.

Walt left to man his booth, so Nina took the girls to the bouncy house. Livvy took her shoes off and slipped them into one of the cubbies provided.

"My friend Baily had one of these at her birthday party. It was cool."

Georgie kicked off her shoes and shoved them in beside her sister's. "Let's go."

"Be careful and watch out for one another."

"We will." The girls disappeared into the large inflated castle, and Nina took up a position where she could see them both. She had to smile at the fun they were having. Livvy did pretty well controlling the bounce, but Georgie kept losing her balance and spent most of her time getting up again.

After a half hour, Livvy made her way to the door and grabbed her shoes. "I want to go help Daddy. He said I could."

Nina hesitated. Separating hadn't been part of the plan. She didn't want to make any mistakes while watching the girls. She had to be super responsible. Her stint as babysitter had gone well, but mainly because they'd all stayed inside and played together the whole time. This was different. This was a large park filled with strangers. "I don't know, Livvy."

"Text him and see, please?"

Bret sent back a quick okay, and Nina watched as Livvy disappeared in the direction of the Phase II tents.

Turning her attention back to Georgie, she saw her and a new friend holding hands as they bounced, and then fell down in a fit of giggles. Confident her charge was safe, Nina took a seat on the bench nearby.

"Ms. Johnson?"

Nina glanced up to see David Ellis, the photographer from the office building, smiling at her. They chatted a few moments, and then he left, and Nina scanned the kids in the bouncy house again. She couldn't locate Georgie. The number of children in the space had doubled, and it was hard to see. She walked close to the side, searching the little heads, but no Georgie. Her heart stopped. The child wasn't inside. Hurrying around to the shoe-storage cubbies, she looked for Georgie's shoes, but they were gone.

Her blood chilled. Air left her lungs, and her pulse raced. Her mind screamed.

"Georgie!" She raced around the house. "Georgie."

*Oh, God, please let me find her.* In the milling crowds, she couldn't see a little girl in a bright red dress. Her mind started to envision terrifying possibilities. What if someone had taken her? What if she'd run off and gotten hurt? Bret would never forgive her. She'd never forgive herself. She'd failed to protect her own child, and now she'd failed to keep Bret's child safe, as well.

Nina ran her fingers up into her hair. Where would she go? She jogged around to the back of the house, where she could see the tent where Walt was working. No Georgie. Beyond that was the fish pond and the adopt-a-pet pen where Deb had her three litters of puppies.

As she hurried toward it, she saw a dark ponytail and a little girl in a red dress sitting on the grass with three puppies in her lap.

Her knees gave way, and she had to grab the trunk of a tree to stay upright. *Thank You, Lord.* Inhaling a deep breath, she set her jaw and started toward the dogs. "Georgie, what are you doing here?"

The little girl looked up, guilt and remorse clearly revealed on her face. "I wanted to see the puppies."

"Why didn't you ask me? I would have brought you over here."

"You were talking to someone."

"That doesn't matter. You don't run off without telling anyone. I'm responsible for you, and I was scared to death. I was afraid something awful had happened to you."

Her lower lip poked out. "I'm sorry."

Now that the crisis was over, Nina's insides were starting to tremble. She had to take the child back to her dad. She couldn't be responsible any longer. Her hands began to shake. "Come on, Georgie. I'm taking you back to your dad."

Georgie slipped her hand in Nina's, and the small little fingers felt like silk. She wanted to squeeze them tight to make sure she didn't get away again.

Bret must have noticed something was wrong, because the moment he saw them, he hurried forward.

"What happened?" Georgie released Nina's hand and ran to her daddy.

Nina found it hard to speak. How could she tell him she'd lost track of his child, even for a few moments?

"I left the bouncy house and didn't tell Miss Nina."

Bret frowned and took her shoulders in his hands and hunkered down. "We've talked about this. You can't go off without letting people know."

"I'm sorry." She glanced over her shoulder at Nina. "I'm sorry."

Bret pointed at the stool behind the display table. "You go sit down."

Nina wrapped her arms around her waist, bracing herself for Bret's anger. How he must hate her. "I only took my eyes off her for a moment. Her shoes were gone, and I didn't see her anywhere. I'm so sorry. I should have been more aware. I should have known better. I've already failed to keep one child safe."

Bret came and took her shoulders in his strong hands, much the same as he had with

Georgie a moment ago. His touch scrubbed off the edge of her panic.

"Hey. Stop. Don't worry about it. It wasn't your fault."

She nodded. "Yes, it was." He didn't understand.

"She does this. She sees something, and off she goes. Where did you find her?"

"With the puppies."

Bret rubbed his forehead. "I might have known. I should have had Dad take her there first."

"I should have watched closer. I shouldn't have spoken to David. I got distracted."

"Stop." He slipped an arm around her shoulders. "Don't beat yourself up. Please. It takes Dad and I both, sometimes, to keep an eye on her. I should have warned you."

The stress was taking its toll. She was sweating. Her heart beat so fiercely, it hurt, and all she wanted was to go home and be someplace safe. "I'm sorry, but I have to leave. I can't stay here."

"Please, don't go. I need you here today. Things are going better than expected. Please." He walked her toward the enclosed tent set up for the Q&A. Inside, he closed the canvas door cover and led her to one of the chairs. He then pulled a bottle of water from the small cooler. "Here, this will help. I know how dry you get after something like this."

"Bret, I'm so sorry. I don't know what to say. You must be so angry." Tears formed in her eyes, and she could do nothing to stop them.

He took her hand and squeezed it. "No. I'm sorry I didn't warn you. I'm not angry. I'm ready to throttle my daughter, but I'm not upset with you."

He touched the side of her face, his thumb gently wiping the tears away. "Did you scold her when you found her?"

She pressed her lips together. Another misstep. "Yes."

"Good. She should have her little nose pinched off. Maybe I'll tell Deb to keep her dog."

"Oh, no. That would break her heart."

Bret smiled. "You're something. As upset as you are, you want my little truant to be happy."

Bret looked into her eyes, and she saw a light come to life. She couldn't deny any longer that she found this man compelling. She was growing fonder and fonder of him. His gaze dropped to her mouth, and her pulse skipped. His head lowered, and she was mesmerized by the thought of his lips on hers.

But he drew back. A strange look on his face. The light in his eyes extinguished.

"The Q&A is starting soon. Will you stay and handle that? If you still want to leave afterward, I'll take you home."

"All right."

She watched him leave, disappointment and confusion replacing much of the fear and regret over Georgie. Why had he pulled away? There was no denying the sparks between them, but he hadn't followed through. Probably because he couldn't afford to get involved with a woman who was so careless with his child.

No, there was something else. Something that erected a barrier between them. He'd been acting strangely for a while. Whatever it was had him deeply troubled. She only hoped he'd open up and share with her. She wanted to help him. In a purely professional way, of course.

## *Chapter Nine*

Bret strolled back to the display table, his thoughts bouncing around like the kids in the inflatable. What had come over him? Had he completely lost his sanity? He'd almost kissed Nina. Heat shot up through his chest. Did he have no moral compass at all? She was Norm's wife, his widow, and it was because of him. He ran a hand down the back of his neck as a different kind of warmth spread through him. God forgive him, he was falling for Nina, and he had no idea how to stop it. He told himself every day that it was wrong, inappropriate and twisted. But every moment with the lovely Nina only made him care more.

She'd been so apologetic when she explained about losing Georgie. The look in her eyes revealed the depth of her affection for his child. He knew that feeling of helplessness only too well. He'd lost track of the little munchkin more times than he'd care to count.

"Hey, fellas. It's time for our first Q&A." The tall blonde woman smiled at them.

"Hi, Leslie. Are you ready for this?"

"Absolutely. I think it was a fabulous idea. I even wore my best artificial hand."

Alan joined her and gave her a quick hug. "We're going to be a great act."

"I hope so."

"We'll see you after the big show." Alan bobbed his eyebrows and headed toward the tent.

Bret turned his attention to the table. The crowds were increasing. He'd have to set aside his concerns for now. But tonight he had to tell Nina the truth. He'd put it off too long. Once she knew, she'd be so angry, she'd probably return to Chicago. The thought was like a knife in his heart, but it was for the best. He couldn't keep silent any longer.

Bret handed out a brochure and gave his speech to a couple who stopped by, forcing a smile he didn't feel.

The afternoon passed quickly. They'd actually run out of brochures, and the Q&A had been a success. Unfortunately, he'd seen Nina slip away after the first session, and he was too busy to go after her. He knew she was still hurting. She cared deeply. But he knew there was more going on. He'd ask her about it soon. Walt had taken the girls home hours ago, and Leslie and Alan offered to tear down the display.

His heart lodged in his throat a short while later when he waited for Nina to answer her door. He didn't want to tell her. Not because it would mean the end of any hope he had of claiming her love, but because it would push her back into that closed room she'd lived in for so long. He loved watching her come out of the darkness. But she was still fragile. If not, she wouldn't have been so quick to blame herself for Georgie's running off.

The door opened, and Nina's eyes lit up as if she were glad to see him. His gut kicked when he realized that wouldn't last long.

"I wanted to see if you were all right. You didn't say goodbye when you left the park."

She stepped aside so he could enter. "I'm sorry. But I had to get away. I needed to think, and I couldn't do that at the park. I kept thinking about what might have happened to Georgie."

He touched her shoulder. "Please, I told you that wasn't your fault."

She stepped out of his reach and crossed

her arms over her chest. "Would you like some coffee?"

"Sure. Thanks." A cup of caffeine would be beneficial to his courage.

He took a seat at her small dining room table. *Lord, give me guidance and courage.*

After she served the coffee, she joined him. "How's Georgie?"

"She's great. Dad took her to see the puppies before they left, and now she's asking for a whole litter for her birthday."

Nina giggled. "I should have guessed."

She was so beautiful when she was happy. If only he could let her be that way forever.

He searched for the words to start, but the only thing that came out was a question. "What did you mean about failing to protect one child?" Her smile vanished, and he kicked himself mentally for being such a dunce. "I'm sorry. I shouldn't have asked."

She drew one leg up onto the chair seat and hugged it with one arm. "That's okay. You have a right to know."

She took a moment to collect her thoughts. "I was taking Molly to a birthday party at her best friend's house. I would always check the child safety lock on the doors, but I was in a hurry that day, and I didn't. When we pulled up at the house, a car had stopped in front of us and I guess she thought we were in the driveway or something. She opened the door and got out and ran across the street, right into the path of a car."

Bret's insides twisted into a knot. His heart broke for her. He couldn't even begin to imagine. He reached across the table for her hand, but she snatched it away. "I'm so sorry."

"I should have checked. I should have paid more attention."

Now he understood why Nina had built such an impenetrable barrier around herself. Losing her child, blaming herself, and then losing her husband, was more grief than one person should have to endure.

His own guilt swelled inside. He couldn't tell her now. He couldn't inflict more pain.

"It was an accident. It wasn't your fault."

"I was her mother. I was supposed to protect her. I never drove after that. Sitting behind the wheel was like reliving the accident all over again." She looked away, staring down at her coffee cup. "I'd like to be alone, if you don't mind."

He didn't want to leave her like this, but he had nothing to offer except more heartache. Now wasn't the time to come clean. He stood up, walked toward her and bent down to place a light kiss on her forehead. "I'll give you a call later." She nodded but didn't reply.

He hesitated, and then he walked out. Maybe he wasn't supposed to tell Nina the truth. Maybe she would be better off if she finished her job here and went back home, never knowing that the man she thought was a friend wasn't.

Nina closed the dishwasher door, pushed Start and then retreated to the front porch with her glass of sweet tea. She was a new convert to the beverage. So many things she'd grown to love about the Deep South. The weather, the food, the easy pace and the people. She'd made friends, shed her hermit-like existence and found a measure of peace. Thanks to her fellow widows and Dottie.

And Bret.

He'd left quickly after she'd explained about Molly. She'd asked him to leave, but he hadn't resisted. No doubt he couldn't stand the sight of her now. In his eyes, she was a neglectful mother, the same as his ex. She hadn't seen him at work today, though Alan had popped in to tell her the veterans' event had been a huge success and the phones were ringing constantly. He claimed it was the Q&A that had made the difference and wanted to give her full credit for the idea.

She had to admit, it was a fascinating session. Alan and Leslie's playful banter had made even the most awkward questions easy. They'd talked about how their artificial limbs were not as good as the real ones, but still allowed them to do everything they used to do. It was a modern marvel that a limb could be replaced with one that worked like the original. But you couldn't do that with a child. You couldn't lose one and simply plug in a new one.

Her mind filled with images of Livvy and Georgie. Though if anything could come close, it would be having those two little princesses in her life. At one point during her babysitting stint, Livvy had asked her to brush her hair. Not for any reason, but so she could sit on Nina's lap. The slow rhythmic strokes soothed the little girl and Nina, too. Molly had been an independent child and always wanted to do things herself. It was nice to have Livvy in her lap. She doubted there would be any more visits now. She'd miss them. All of them. Even the matchmaking Walt.

She became aware that darkness had blanketed the neighborhood. Lights began to appear in the homes along her street. Fatigue settled heavily on her shoulders. Maybe it would be wise to turn in early tonight. She had a full schedule of patients tomorrow and the group therapy with the widows. She locked up, turned off the lights and padded down the hall to the bedroom.

A loud crash split the silence.

She froze. Had something fallen? Ted was working on the other apartments, but he never worked in the evenings. Should she go and see? It really wasn't her concern, but Ted had been generous. The least she could do was check on his property. It was probably nothing more than a fallen board.

A scraping sound came from the hallway. Her heart raced. Perhaps a stray cat or dog had gotten inside and was nosing around. Tiptoeing to the front door, she slowly opened it just enough to peek out. Her heart stopped. There in the shadows, at the end of the hall, were two men carrying boxes out the back door. One of them returned and picked up strips of wood from the pile and dragged them out.

She eased the door closed, trying to think. *Call the police.* She fumbled for her phone and managed to get a message through to the local police, but she derived little comfort from the action. How quickly could they get here? Would they be too late? A shiver chased down her spine. What if the thieves discovered she was inside the house? Would they rob her, too, or worse? Her fingers danced over her phone screen as she waited anxiously to hear Bret's calm, reassuring voice.

She cupped her hand over the phone and spoke softly. "Bret. There are men outside in the hall stealing the construction stuff. I've called the police, but I'm scared."

"Go hide in the bedroom or bathroom. Keep quiet. I'll be right there."

The odd sounds from the hall repeated several times, but Nina stayed in the bedroom. When a loud knock sounded on the door, she jumped.

"Hastings police."

She hurried to the door and looked through the peephole. A uniformed officer stood there. She eased the door open slowly.

"Are you Ms. Johnson?"

Before she could say anything, Bret appeared, stepping around the officer and pulling her close. "Are you all right?"

She clung to him, realizing just how frightened she'd been and feeling the fear melt away in his nearness.

After she spoke with the officer and gave him a description of the men, Bret guided her inside her apartment. He took her shoulders in his hands. "I don't think you should stay here tonight. Put a few things together, and you can spend the night at my house."

Her first instinct was to remain in her own place, but the thought of those men returning was too frightening. "Okay. Give me a few minutes." She got dressed, packed clothes for work the next day, filled her cosmetic bag and then hurried back to the front room. "I'm ready."

"I'm glad you called me."

"I'm glad you came. Having you here made me feel safe and protected." She blushed. That was far too intimate a thing to say to a man in the middle of the night. "I mean, I called the police first, but then…" She fumbled for words.

Bret smiled, his green eyes filled with tenderness. "It always helps to have a friend beside you in times of trouble."

She took one last glance around. She loved her little apartment and the cozy home it had become. The thought of someone breaking in, stealing or destroying her belongings, left a knot in the center of her chest. "Do you think they'll come back?"

"Doubtful, but I'd feel better if you were with me. I don't want anything to happen to you."

Ted appeared in the hall as Bret and Nina were leaving. He'd already spoken to the police, who were still collecting evidence.

"Are you okay? I'm so sorry about this. I've had materials stolen before, but never from inside an occupied dwelling."

Nina reassured him she was fine, but worried about the tiles and lumber that had been stolen. He waved off her concern and assured her that his insurance would cover it.

"I'm going to get a night watchman to be on the premises. You won't have to worry about this happening again."

Bret's house was quiet when they arrived. They entered through the back door to the dimly lit kitchen. Walt was sitting at the table with a cup of coffee. He smiled when he saw her.

"I knew you'd be coming out here. I've got the spare room all ready for ya. Didn't have any mints for the pillow, though, so you'll just have to tough it out."

His comment made her smile. "Thank you. I appreciate you letting me stay."

Bret set her suitcase on the floor. "I didn't mean for you to stay awake, Dad. I just wanted you to know what was going on."

"I know, but I wasn't going to sleep until I knew our little lady was safe and sound."

Nina's heart warmed. Was that how Walt thought of her? And what about Bret? How did he think of her? Or did he think of her at all?

Walt set a cup of hot tea on the table and motioned for her to sit. "You drink that, and you'll sleep like a baby." He winked, and then he left the room.

Bret joined her at the table and laid a hand on hers. "Feeling better?"

She nodded and took a sip of the soothing tea. "Much. Thank you for letting me stay with you." She glanced away, aware of how her words could be interpreted. Quickly, she searched for another topic of conversation. "Have you made a decision about the girls' mother coming to see them?"

"Yeah. She's coming to see them in a few days." He wrapped his hands around the glass of iced tea he was drinking. "I did take your advice, and I talked to the girls the other night about their mother."

"Did they tell you anything?"

"Not really. Georgie doesn't remember her at all, and Livvy didn't seem upset or even curious about her mother."

Nina squeezed his hand. "I'm not surprised. From what I can see, the girls are happy and well-adjusted. You're doing a great job."

"Am I? I wish I could believe that. They need a mother. A woman to counter Dad and me."

"Maybe one day you'll find her."

His eyes were shadowed and sad when he met her gaze. "No. I don't think that will happen now."

Nina mulled that statement over in her head as she drifted off to sleep later. What had he meant? Something was definitely troubling him, and she wished he'd let her help.

Bret poured orange juice in each of the girls' glasses, and then stepped aside as his dad scooped fresh pancakes onto their plates. "Eat up, girls. It's almost time to leave for school."

"Can we stay home today and play with Miss Nina?"

"No. Besides, she has to go to work like I do. Maybe you'll see her at dinner tonight." At least he hoped so. Nina had been here for two nights, and he found himself wishing it could be more. He liked having her in his home. She brought sunshine and warmth into the old rooms. The girls vied for her attention, taking turns sitting on her lap or snuggling up with a book for her to read to them. She enjoyed it, too. He could see it in the sparkle in her eyes and the way she smiled and laughed all the time. She must have been a wonderful mom.

"Good morning." Nina came into the kitchen and went straight to Olivia and gave her a kiss on the top of her head. "Did you sleep well, sweetheart?"

Olivia nodded, a big smile on her face. "I dreamed about you and me on a picnic."

"That sounds like fun. Georgie, did you have sweet dreams?"

Georgie wiggled, stood up in her chair and opened her arms to Nina. "I dreamed about lots and lots of puppies."

Nina turned and joined Walt at the stove, giving him an affectionate pat on the back. Bret marveled at how easily she fit into his life. Finally she turned and looked at him, her blue eyes warm and affectionate. "Good morning, Bret."

His heart thudded in his chest. "I hope you slept well, too. Things here aren't as calm and quiet as at your place."

"But it's much more entertaining."

"Speaking of your place, Ted called and said it's safe for you to go home. The thieves have been captured. He's hired a watchman, and the police will be doubling their patrols in the neighborhood."

"Oh, good. I'm so relieved."

Was she disappointed to be leaving his home? He wanted her to be, but he couldn't blame her for wanting to be back in her own place. "I'll drop you off after work today." The light in her blue eyes clouded.

"Okay. Thank you."

Bret wanted to believe he saw regret in her eyes, a glint of sadness at leaving, but he shouldn't. It would only make the end of this relationship more painful. And it would end. He was determined not to let another week go by without revealing his secret. He had to stop this fantasy about a life with Nina and face facts. Soon.

Walt clapped his hands to get the girls' attention. "Okey-dokey. Time to get moving. Get your gear, and let's head to the car. We don't want to be late for school." A round of hugs and kisses followed, and then the trio disappeared out the back door, leaving him alone with Nina in the kitchen.

Their gazes locked. The pull between them vibrated. Was she thinking the same thing he was? That they could share every morning like this? Together as a family?

Nina abruptly turned away. "I'd better get ready for work and pack my things." She hurried from the room, leaving him wondering what she was thinking.

* * *

Nina stepped into the main hall of the old house that evening. Visions of the thieves slipping out the back door flashed across her mind. She gripped the key to her apartment and swallowed hard. Bret spoke from behind her, where he'd kept his hand lightly against the small of her back as they'd entered the old house.

"It's all right. There are new locks on all the doors, a watchman and increased patrols, but if you'd like to stay with us a little longer, you can."

Part of her wanted to turn and run back to his house, but that was her childish fear talking. "No. I'm ready to be home." She turned the key and went inside. Relief washed over her, and a sense of peace welcomed her home. Nothing had changed. Her little home was untouched. Yet a small memory surfaced of the love and closeness she'd experienced at Bret's. It was nice to have someone at home waiting for you. She felt comfortable in his home and in his life. Waking up in his home, with the smell of breakfast in the air, and seeing the girls' sweet faces, made the mornings special. The sight of their father rumpled, barefoot and totally male was an added perk.

Bret put her small suitcase in the bedroom,

and then returned to the living room. "How does it feel to be home again?"

She smiled. He was such a sweet man. "Good. I'm ready to curl up on the sofa and relax all evening. But I have to admit, I got used to all the activity at your place. It feels a bit lonely in here."

A big smile spread across his handsome face, and his green eyes lit up. "I may have a solution to that problem. Wait right there, and no peeking. I'll be right back."

He hurried out, and Nina stared at the door. No peeking? What did that mean? He came through the door a few moments later with a little dog on a leash. A large pink bow was tied around her neck. She recognized it as the one who had befriended her the day they'd picked out Georgie's puppy. The furry little bundle came to her immediately and placed her front paws on Nina's legs, begging to be petted.

"Oh, it's the dog from the farm." Her heart melted, and she scooped up the furry critter and cuddled her close. "Did you change your mind and get her for Georgie?"

"No. I got her for you. She's your new watchdog, your burglar alarm and, in her spare time, a companion to chase away the lonely."

"For me?" No one else but Bret would

think of something so thoughtful. The dog licked her neck, eliciting a giggle. "You are so sweet." The little dog fit perfectly in her arms.

"Deb said her name is Sadie, but you can change it. Just keep repeating the new name until she responds. But she also said, if you aren't ready for a dog, you can bring her back. I know I sprung it on you without asking."

"No. I love her. I seriously thought about taking her that day at the farm, but I didn't know if Ted would allow it. Have you asked him?"

"He's behind it all the way. A dog on the premises is a great deterrent to intruders."

Nina hugged the fuzzy thing closer, digging her fingertips into his thick buff-colored fur. Her gaze sought his. "You've become my personal protector. Standing up to the irate husband, rescuing me from thieves and now giving me a watchdog."

"I'm no protector. I just don't want anything to happen to you. You're very important to me, Nina."

The soft, intimate tone of his voice, and the tender look in his eyes, sent a rush of warmth along her arms and neck. Maybe it was time to stop pretending and admit that Bret was someone she could care about deeply. But she shouldn't. She wasn't the kind of woman he needed.

Gathering her senses, she put the dog down and realized something important. "Oh, Bret, I don't have a dog bed or food or bowls for her."

"I took care of that, too." He hurried back outside and returned with the necessary dog paraphernalia.

"Where were you keeping the dog and all this stuff?"

He grinned and shrugged. "Deb is outside. She met me here."

"Invite her in."

"She said she'd stop later and answer any questions you might have." He scratched the dog's neck a moment, and then he straightened. "I'd better go. I know you're anxious to get back to normal. At least I feel better about you being here with that mutt to sound the alarm."

"Bret, it was a wonderful gift. Thank you so much." Without thinking, she rested her palm on his chest. She could feel his heart beating. It was perfectly in time with her own. She started to pull away, but he laid his large hand over hers, pinning it to him.

His other hand slipped behind her back, urging her closer. She knew she should resist, but it was impossible. He was going to kiss her, and she wasn't going to stop him. She'd wondered too long what it would be like, and now she was going to know. Their gazes locked, and Nina leaned in, her arms slipping around his neck and her fingertips slipping into the silky strands of his dark hair.

His lips covered hers, and she melted against him, lost in the sensation and the taste of him. His kiss was firm but gentle, and he slowly kissed her more deeply, more confidently. All her senses were swirling. A sensation of being whole and complete again swelled in her core, leaving behind a feeling of being renewed and free.

He ended the kiss, and the cool air rushed in between them. She looked into his eyes, and for a brief moment, she saw her own emotions reflected in the green depths. But then it faded, and his eyes became dull and murky.

He set her away, shaking his head slowly. "I'm sorry. I never meant for that to happen. It's wrong and inappropriate and…" He pivoted and walked out, closing the door firmly behind him.

Stunned, she could only stare at the door, her mind twisted with confusion and pain. What did he mean? He'd said he was sorry. He said the kiss was inappropriate. Why? Because he didn't care for her that way, or because she was all wrong for him?

She covered her face with her hands, humiliation flaming along her skin. She should have resisted, not let it happen, but she'd wanted to kiss him more than anything in that moment.

She wished now that he hadn't kissed her. She would cherish the memory, but that was all it could be. Tears stung the backs of her eyes. What could she do about her heart? She was falling in love with this special man. Despite her resolve, he'd slipped past her barrier. But her feelings were futile. Bret would never risk his heart again, or those of his daughters. He was sorry he'd kissed her because he could never have real feelings for her. The attraction might be there, but that was all it would ever be.

She picked up Sadie and cuddled with her on the couch, taking comfort from the warm little body. Sadie was exactly what she needed. Besides, kissing Bret was her fault. She should have been stronger.

From now on, she'd be an iron woman. Her only focus would be her job and her new pet.

## *Chapter Ten*

Bret drove away from Nina's house, made the corner and pulled to a stop at the curb. He pinched the bridge of his nose. A protector. He wasn't a protector. He couldn't protect her husband from being killed, or his girls from losing their mother. Worst of all, he couldn't protect Nina from himself. He should have turned away; he should never have kissed her.

The look in her eyes was so soft and appealing, her small hand had rested against his chest, and the contact had shot through him like a bullet. He'd lost control. All that mattered was holding her and satisfying his curiosity about how her lips would feel and taste. It had been more than he'd ever imagined. Her kiss was sweet, warm and wrapped around him like a fragrant spring breeze. And she'd kissed him back, answering the other question that had dogged him. She cared about him, too.

He exhaled a sigh. All he was doing was digging his hole deeper, because when she found out the truth, that look of affection and longing in her eyes would turn to hate.

Bret pulled away from the curb and turned the vehicle toward home. He had some hard thinking to do, as well as some serious praying. He hadn't done much of that lately. He had a bad habit of letting his prayer time go when he was busy or troubled, thinking he could somehow work it all out on his own. He knew better. Those were the times he should be praying more.

His dad was waiting in the rocker on the front porch when he arrived home.

"Did she like the dog?"

Bret nodded, lowering himself into the rocker beside his dad. "Yeah, she did."

"But something didn't go right. What was it?"

"Nothing. I just lost my head, that's all."

"I think I can translate that." He closed the magazine he was reading and leaned toward his son. "That young woman is a good fit for you, son. A good fit for all of us. You know that, don't you?"

"Not after she learns the truth."

"You can't let her slip away, or you'll regret it for the rest of your life. You need to end this. Do the right thing, and the Lord will work out the rest."

Bret knew his dad was right. The Lord would work things out, but that didn't mean they'd work out the way Bret wanted. From his perspective, there was no scenario he'd envisioned that ended on a happy note. But he couldn't continue the way he was. Growing more and more in love, yet knowing he was withholding vital information.

No matter how painful it would be, he had to come clean and trust that Nina was strong enough now to handle the truth. He would arrange to meet her in the next few days. No excuses or delays.

But he had a pretty good idea of how things would end. She would return to Chicago, and his heart would eventually heal. Or would it?

The skies were overcast, blocking the sunshine the next afternoon as he watched Sylvia's car pull up in front of his house. The gloomy weather was fitting for what was about to take place. He'd agreed to let Sylvia see the girls, but wasn't at all sure it was a good idea.

He opened the door and acknowledged her

with a silent nod, his throat too constricted to say her name. She looked different. Not only was she much thinner than he remembered, but her hair was a lighter color, and her makeup heavier than he'd ever seen. There was little left of the woman he had married.

He shut the door behind her, and then he went and stood with Olivia and Georgie, resting a protective hand on each small shoulder. His insides were tied in painful knots. Had he made another bad decision letting her see the children? He had no idea what to expect. The girls hadn't expressed any interest in seeing her when he told them she was coming. Now they stood stiff, cautiously staring at the woman across the room. He cleared his throat.

Sylvia took a few steps forward. "Hello, girls. You've grown so much since I last saw you."

Bret nudged his daughters. "What do you say?"

"Hello."

Sylvia lifted her chin. "I'd like to speak to the girls alone, please."

Bret hesitated. What would Nina advise him to do? "Fine, but only for a few minutes. You can use the living room, but I'll be close by."

"Come on, girls. Let's have a visit." She

held out her hands to them, but they ignored the gesture and walked slowly into the living room, leaving Bret with a sick feeling in his stomach. *Please, Lord, don't let this meeting upset my daughters.*

Barely five minutes later, the girls came out and pressed against his side. He hugged them close.

Olivia looked up at him with sad eyes. "Can we go be with Grandpa now?"

"Of course. Take your sister with you."

Olivia took Georgie's hand and started away. He heard his youngest murmur she wished Miss Nina was here.

"Bret."

He pivoted to see Sylvia staring at him, her expression one of sadness.

"I'm sorry. I shouldn't have come. I didn't expect the girls not to know me. Stupid. I should have."

He set his jaw. "You haven't been part of their lives for a long time."

She nodded. "I won't try and see them again. It's best for everyone. Bret, I want you to know that you weren't at fault in any of this. I'm just not cut out for the marriage-and-kids thing. It wasn't because you were deployed, or because of anything you failed to do as a husband. It was all me. I don't want you blaming yourself. There was nothing you could have done, okay."

He nodded. A strange lightening circled his heart. "I hope you'll find what makes you happy."

"I'm trying." She inhaled a deep breath and moved toward the door. "You're doing a good job with our daughters. Thank you for that. Goodbye."

Bret shut the door behind Sylvia, and then he ran a hand through his hair. All the tension he'd held over her visit had vanished. He'd anticipated a disaster and upset children. Instead, he'd been given a form of release. He no longer had to blame himself for his failed marriage. He was free now to move forward with his life.

But first he had to check with the girls and make sure they were okay. He smiled as he thought about telling Nina about the visit. She'd been right. Letting the girls see their mother would give them all a form of closure.

Nina curled up on the sofa, her gaze riveted on Bret. He'd asked if he could come over to talk. He'd already shared with her the details of the visit with the girls' mother, and she'd been pleased to hear it had all gone well, with no ill effects on the children. But whatever it was on his mind was causing him to struggle to find words. She bit her lip. Her throat tightened. What could he possibly have to tell her that upset him so deeply? His green eyes were dark and troubled, which only made her more anxious.

"Nina, I want to talk about your husband."

That wasn't what she'd expected. "Chip? Why?"

Bret rubbed his forehead. "I want to tell… I need to let you know…" He sighed and pressed his palms together. "Just tell me about him. Were you close? I mean, was your marriage a good one?"

"Yes. Very good, until Molly's death. Why do you need to know?"

"I'm curious. You never talk about him, and when you do, it makes you agitated and angry. I thought talking about it might help you, and since we're friends, I wanted to offer my ear."

She studied him. He appeared sincere and earnest. And he was right. Talking did help, and she'd been fighting the emotions that had started to rise to the surface. What would it hurt? And it might help. "We had a good marriage. He was an ordained minister, but he found his calling as a professor of religious studies at a Christian college."

"I thought you said he died in the Middle East."

"He did. That was after... The three of us did everything together. He adored Molly.

"When she died, it tore us apart. He said he didn't blame me, but I could see it in his eyes every time he looked at me. Everyone blamed me, even my mother. But no one more than me.

"I thought we'd eventually work things out, but then Chip announced he had requested reinstatement from reserves to active duty. He said he felt a calling from the Lord to go and help the soldiers as a chaplain again. But I knew the real reason. He couldn't stand to be around me. He was running away, as far as he could."

"I doubt that."

"It's true. He said he needed the distance so he could reevaluate his life, and that helping others would help him restore his faith. Never mind that I needed him with me." Old pain and resentment rushed to the surface, bringing hot tears to her eyes. This was a bad idea. She wasn't ready to face this part of her past.

"I'm sorry."

But now that she was talking, she couldn't stop. "If that wasn't bad enough, he was supposed to be protected by another soldier, but instead he was killed. If he'd stayed home, he would have been safe." She brushed tears from her cheeks. "He hated me so much that he had to go halfway around the world to find peace. I never realized until then how much he despised me."

"No. That's not true. He adored you. He talked about you all the time. He didn't blame you at all."

Nina froze. Conflicting emotions pressed against her chest and up into her throat. What was he saying? "How do you know what my husband felt? How could you possibly know that?"

Bret stood abruptly and ran his fingers along his scalp as he turned his back.

"Bret. I want an explanation." She saw his shoulders sag and his head bow. When he faced her again, the agony in his green eyes frightened her.

"My last assignment before I separated was as a chaplain's assistant."

Nina sorted out the words, trying to make sense. Chip had an assistant. A soldier whose only job was to keep him safe. But what did that have to do with Bret? It still wasn't making sense.

Bret inhaled a deep breath and squared his shoulders. "I was assigned to Chaplain Norman Grant."

Like molasses dripping slowly off a spoon, the truth hit. A voice inside her head screamed. Her heart pounded. She stared at Bret, trying to align the man she'd come to know with the hated soldier she'd envisioned all these years. "You. You got my husband killed?"

Hot, scalding fury exploded inside her being. She stood and marched toward him. "You were supposed to keep him safe. You were his shield."

"I know. I'm sorry."

Her hands curled into tight fists. "Sorry? That's not good enough."

"Nina, it isn't what you think. I'd like to tell you how it happened."

"I know how it happened. You didn't do your job."

"Don't you think I know that?"

Nina turned her back. She didn't want to hear how he felt. "How long have you known?"

"Since the day I saw the picture of you and your husband in your apartment. I've been trying to tell you for a while, but I could never find the right time."

Her mind refused to process the information. "All this time you've been hiding it from me while you pretended to be my friend. Why?"

"I am your friend. Please, let me explain."

She waved her hand in the air for him to stop talking. A million questions swirled in her mind, each demanding an answer. "Why didn't you contact me after he died? Why didn't you let me know then?"

"I tried, but you never answered."

That was probably true. She'd refused to read anything that had come through official channels those first six months. "You should have tried harder."

"You're right. But you have to understand I was devastated by his death. Yes, I was supposed to protect him. Yes, I failed. I didn't know how to handle that. I loved the chaplain. He was the finest man I'd ever met."

"How nice for you."

"Nina, he brought me back to the Lord. I owe him. He saved me. Yet I wasn't able to save him. I couldn't face myself after that."

Nina steeled her heart against the agony in his voice.

"Before I could come to terms with Norm's

death, I got word about my wife walking out. After that, all I could think about was my girls. I got home to them as soon as I could. But I carried my failure with Norm on my shoulders. I still do."

She clenched her jaw. "Good. You should. I hope you carry it forever."

"Nina, please. Norm loved you. He regretted leaving you. All he talked about was getting home again so he could make things right. But, Nina, he was a great chaplain. He gave comfort to so many. He was an amazing human being."

Nina didn't want to hear that right now. Bret was shredding everything she'd thought she knew about Chip and his death. "You need to leave. Now."

"Nina. I want to tell you how it happened. It might help you see…"

"No. I don't want to hear how he died. None of it. Why would you think that?"

Bret's shoulders sagged. "All right. I'll go, but we need to talk about this more later on."

"Never. I don't want to talk to you ever again."

Bret opened his mouth to say something, but then closed it again. Without a word, he pivoted and left, closing the front door softly behind him.

Nina fought the tears as they stung her eyes. Wrapping her arms around her waist, she stumbled to the sofa and sank into it. She curled up with a pillow as the sobs escaped her throat. Sadie curled up at her feet, offering comfort.

Bret. Bret was the man to blame for Chip's death. How was this possible? It was too incredible to grasp. Why hadn't she known? Because she'd crawled into a cave after Chip left and refused to acknowledge his existence. She'd deleted Chip's emails and ignored any attempts to set up live chats. He'd written, but she'd never opened the letters, and they had eventually stopped coming. Her hurt was too deep. Losing Molly, and then Chip, had been a trauma so profound, the only way to survive was to close off the world and pretend it never happened. Chip could very well have told her about Bret. Especially since they had grown close, but she didn't want to hear about his time overseas. If he'd rather go off to a war zone than stay with her when she needed him, then so be it. She didn't need him. She didn't need anyone.

How could she move forward now? How could she ever erase the image of Chip lying dead because Bret had failed him?

It shouldn't matter. Except for the fact that

her heart was drawn to Bret. He'd become a big part of her life here in Hastings. Not only him, but Walt and the girls. But how could she have deep affection for the man who got her husband killed? She'd lost everything partly because of him.

No. It had all started with her neglect. She was to blame for the chain of events. No one else.

The pressure inside his chest threatened to crack his ribs. He'd blown it. Handled the situation completely wrong. He'd imagined telling Nina the truth a hundred times, but it had never played out like this.

He'd been careless and spoke without considering his words. He'd wanted to sit with Nina quietly, calmly, and tell her gently who he was and what he'd failed to do. Instead, he'd thrown the truth in her face.

The friendly light in her pretty eyes had turned into an angry storm as the shock and horror of the truth sunk in. She'd pulled away, throwing up that old barrier and shutting herself down. He should have told her sooner, but he was too afraid of the consequences. The truth was he'd been attracted to Nina from the start—long before he'd met her in front of the building.

He'd hurt her deeply, and she'd never forgive him. His mind scrolled through all the things that would change between them now. No more quick conversations at the office, she'd never set foot in his home again, his girls would never see her and she might even pull up stakes and walk away from the practice, and he couldn't blame her one bit.

Worst of all, he knew how she felt. He'd experienced all the same emotions when Sylvia had walked out. Betrayed, duped, scraped raw. He'd called himself all kinds of a fool for not knowing, not suspecting. He'd felt like a failure and a blind dunce, too trusting to see what was right in front of him.

Walt had a fresh pot of coffee and a piece of hot blueberry cobbler waiting for Bret when he got home. He wasn't in the mood to eat, but the aroma was tempting. The cobbler was a touch point between father and son. Whenever something serious needed to be discussed, his mom would bake one, and then settle them at the table to talk things over.

"I take it things didn't go so well." Walt set a plate of cobbler in front of Bret and took a seat.

"You'd be correct. I messed it up."

"How so?"

"It doesn't matter. She's angry, and I can't blame her."

"Give her some time. It must have been a shock."

Bret nodded, wincing at the memory of the pain in her eyes. "She thought her husband reactivated because he wanted to get away from her."

"Did he?"

"No. He was searching for peace after his child's death. It had nothing to do with Nina, and he regretted leaving. He wanted to get home to her."

"Did you tell her that?"

"She wasn't ready to listen. Now she's hurting and alone, and there's nothing I can do to help."

"Just how much do you care for this woman?"

Bret wrapped his palms around the coffee mug, needing something to hang on to. "I've had feelings for her long before she came to Hastings."

"What do you mean?"

"Chaplain Grant and I were close. We spent every moment together. He talked about his wife. A lot. He'd confided to me that he'd made a mistake returning to active duty. He was glad to be there serving, but he knew he'd left his wife to grieve on her own. He was hurting, unable to process why God had taken his only child. His life was in chaos, and he saw the army as a way to get order and regimen back in his life.

"He missed his wife. He called her 'my girl.' And he told me all about her. How strong she was and how loving, and what a wonderful mother she'd been to their daughter. He spoke of her with such love and adoration—such depth of feeling—that I came to think of her as special, too. The kind of woman I would hope to find someday. I realized I'd married Sylvia in haste. We didn't know each other well, and we tried to build a life.

"The chaplain's wife sounded like perfection. I used to imagine what she looked like. He never said, and he didn't have a picture. He wrote to her, but never got an answer. He never got upset with her, only said she was still hurting, and when he got home, he'd make it all up to her. That was his goal. To get home to his girl."

Bret glanced at his dad. "My first thought when he was killed was that I'd failed to get him home to his wife."

"So, you've had a crush on this woman?"

"In a way. I used to encourage him to talk about her, telling myself it would help him, but then I realized it was because I wanted to know all about her. So I stopped asking, and when he brought up the subject, I made excuses to leave. I wasn't proud of my curiosity about her. I was married. She was another man's wife."

Walt nodded. "Understandable. There's no crime in that from afar, as long as you don't act upon it."

"That wasn't an option. And I put all that aside when Sylvia left."

"And you had no idea who she was when she came here?"

"No. Nina isn't that unusual a name, and she was going by her maiden name, Johnson." He poked at the cobbler with his fork. "She didn't look or behave anything like the woman I'd created in my mind. Norm always spoke of her as warm and nurturing, gentle and sweet—the same way Kitty spoke of her friend. But she was stiff and cool and closed off."

"And you didn't suspect until you saw that photo at her place?"

"No." He leaned back in the chair and rubbed his eyes. "I know I should have told her sooner, but it never seemed like the right time or place. Then she started to open up, and I could see glimpses of the woman Norm had talked about, and I wanted to see more. I knew if I told her the truth, she'd retreat back into that shell like a hermit crab."

"And you didn't want to see that happen?"

Bret bristled at his father's implication. "Not for me. For her. She was coming alive again. Her grief was easing up. I didn't want her to lose all the progress she'd made."

"What happens now?"

He shoved the plate of cobbler away. "I don't know."

"Did you tell her the whole story?"

"No. She's not ready for that yet. I'll try to talk to her again in a few days."

"She needs to hear it all, son."

"I know. I promise I won't leave anything out, but…"

"But what? What are you worried about?"

"I've come to have feelings for her. Not the idealized image of her I formed overseas, but real feelings. But now that's all over."

"Maybe not. You can't know that until the whole truth is out."

"No. She'll never see me as anything other than the man who failed to save her husband."

"Maybe, for a time. But she's special. I saw that from the first. I see how she is with you, and how she interacts with the girls. Her feelings are involved, too, son. A lot more than you might think."

Bret shook his head. "Nice try. My track record is poor. I might have picked a winner this time, but I'm also responsible for causing it to fail."

Walt stood and placed a reassuring hand on his shoulder. "I don't believe that. I think Nina is a keeper, and I think it'll all work out in time. Let her take the lead. Once the shock wears off, she'll want to know what happened. She'll come to you and demand answers. Then you tell your story. After that, let the good Lord work out the rest."

"What if He doesn't work it out the way I want?"

"Then He has something better in store for you, no matter how you might feel otherwise." He gave Bret's shoulder a shake. "Remember, I'm good at picking the right woman. I picked your mom, and I picked Nina for you. And I'm not changing my mind unless the Almighty shows me otherwise."

Nina chewed on her bottom lip, struggling to comprehend what she'd just learned. It was too fantastic to be real, but it was. Bret Sinclair was the chaplain's assistance officer who allowed Chip to die.

It would be so easy if she didn't know Bret. He could be just some soldier who failed in his duties. That was the way she'd always thought of him. Until today. He wasn't some macho soldier who messed up. He was a decent, honorable man, a father of two girls he adored, a man who worked hard to serve his fellow veterans and his community.

The two images refused to mesh. Curled on the couch, knees drawn up to her chest, one hand buried in Sadie's fur, she came at the situation from all angles and could find no direction that made sense. She was a therapist. She should know how to handle these things. But the pain was too deep emotionally and too close physically. She needed another opinion. But who? One name surged into her mind.

Reaching for her cell, she dialed a number, praying that the woman would be home and could come to her rescue. The warm hello on the other end of the connection unleashed tears in Nina's eyes. "Dottie. It's me."

"Nina? Sweet thing, what's wrong?"

"Can you come over? I really need someone to talk to. I've just learned something very upsetting, and I don't know how to handle it."

"Of course. I'll be right there."

A half hour later, Dottie had arrived, fixed glasses of sweet tea and had been filled in on the shocking truth.

"You know, if I'd read this plot in a book, I'd never believe it. What are the chances?"

Nina wiped her eyes with a tissue. The tears would not stop falling. "How could he do that? Just let my husband be killed. He was supposed to protect him, even take a bullet for him if necessary."

"Did Bret explain the situation to you? Did he tell you what happened?"

"I didn't give him a chance."

"Don't you think he deserves that much?"

"No. I'm a widow because of him."

"That may be true, but you should hear the whole story. Hear his side of things."

"I don't want to see him."

"You'd rather remain in ignorance, is that it?"

Nina knew she was responding badly, but she didn't care. "No, but I don't think I can stand to look at him."

"I've known Bret a long time. He's one of the most responsible men I know. I can't imagine him being careless about his assignment or anyone under his care. Can you?"

Nina couldn't disagree. Bret *was* responsible. But that didn't negate what had happened. Nina reached for another tissue. "I just need to find a way to handle this. I've looked through all my books and files, searched online, but this isn't something dealt with in training."

Dottie patted her knee. "Maybe that's because you're looking in the wrong places and the wrong books. You know King David went through a lot of painful, hurtful situations. But he came out okay. And what about poor old Job. He knew loss and grief better than anyone."

A rush of heat filled Nina's cheeks. Dottie was right. She'd sent up desperate pleas to the Lord, little cries of help, but she'd never opened her Bible to find the answers. She'd never stopped and allowed herself to listen to what the Lord's answer might be.

Dottie stayed a few minutes longer. Before she left, she gave Nina a hug. "I'm only a phone call away. Holler if you need me."

Nina held the woman close. "You've been such a blessing to me. I'll miss you when I go back home."

"Maybe you should consider staying here. Then you wouldn't have to miss me."

Nina closed the door. Stay here in Hastings? There was no reason. Her secret fantasies about a life with Bret, things she'd barely acknowledged to herself, were shattered now. They were only impossible dreams.

\* \* \*

The widows' therapy session was in chaos. Nina had tried to hide her turmoil over Bret's admission, but the old mask she used to wear no longer worked. She'd spent the last week trying to find the opening to her emotional cave so she could slither back inside, but failed. Too much had happened. She'd changed too much. Hiding from reality was no longer an option. She'd considered canceling the widows' group, but realized she needed the support and encouragement now as much as they did.

She'd welcomed her widows and opened the time for discussion, but the women had seen right through her attempts to hide her pain, and they refused to let her off the hook.

She filled them in as best she could and gave herself over to their advice. Tonight she was the patient in need of counseling, and they were far more equipped on matters of widowhood than she was. In a strange way, it felt good to have friends surrounding her and not be the one in charge with all the answers.

"I can't believe this." Charlotte shook her head. "Of all the gin joints in all the towns."

"No kidding," Paula agreed. "All the soldiers in all the world, and he ends up in the office across the hall. Too weird."

"Did he tell you what happened?" Trudy asked.

"He tried, but I wasn't ready to hear it."

Jen leaned forward. "You said your husband wrote to you. What did he say? Did he mention Bret at all?"

Nina shook her head. "I never read his letters. I was too angry and hurt, and I didn't want to know anything about where he was or what he was doing."

The women all muttered their understanding.

Charlotte spoke up. "I don't know Bret well, but his daughter Olivia is in my class, and she is a sweet child and a good student. He's always struck me as a good man and devoted father. Not someone who would shirk responsibility."

Nina didn't disagree, but that didn't explain things. "Then why didn't he tell me?"

Trudy spoke softly. "Maybe because he was afraid you'd hate him. You know he's in love with you."

Paula leaned back in her seat. "That would explain a lot."

"That must have been hard for him, caring about you, but knowing he'd made you a widow. Talk about a burden."

"I agree, Trudy."

Nina tried to quell her irritation. All the support was for Bret. "Have you forgotten he failed to protect my husband and he died?"

Jen reached out and touched her arm. "No, of course not, but what were the circumstances? What happened that caused it? Was Bret directly responsible? Derelict in his duties? Or was something else going on? You need to find out the whole truth before you can sort this out."

Charlotte nodded in agreement. "Jen has a point. The bottom line is this is all about understanding and forgiveness. Until you know everything, you're only speculating and holding on to the pain and anger."

Nina hated to admit it, but they were right. Once again her widows had given her a new perspective.

As much as she tried to ignore their advice, she knew she had to push past the anger and shock and do what she should have done years ago. Read Chip's letters.

But not yet. Later, when she was stronger.

# *Chapter Eleven*

❧

Nina stepped from the cab and stood on the sidewalk in front of Bret's house. The charming Craftsman cottage suited the little family. It was warm, welcoming and homey. Livvy and Georgie would love growing up here.

Today was Georgie's birthday party. She'd wrestled with the decision whether to come or not for several days. One moment, she'd convince herself that going to the party was a bad idea. It would send the wrong message to Bret. He might think that she was all right with his behavior. Then the next moment, she would think about little Georgie and how much she'd looked forward to her birthday. She couldn't stand the thought of missing her expression when she received her puppy. Besides, she loved the little girl, and her sister, too, so she'd decided to come for their sake. She'd ignore

Bret as much as possible and spend her time with Walt and enjoy the party. The minute the party was over, she would leave. Let Bret draw his own conclusions.

Clutching her gift a little closer, she took a deep breath and started up the walk. Her knock was answered instantly, and Georgie flung her arms around her in a fierce hug.

"I knew you'd come. I told Daddy you would. He said you were too busy, but I knew he was kidding." She turned and hollered inside. "Livvy, she's here. She's here."

Georgie took Nina's hand and tugged her inside. They hurried down the hallway to the back door. The yard had been turned into party central. Streamers and balloons dangled from the trees, the patio cover and any other place that was available. The ornate playhouse had been festooned with ribbons and bows, as well.

A table set off to one side had been reserved for gifts. Georgie took the small present from her hand, muttered a thank-you and raced to the table to place it there. She returned and slipped her little hand in Nina's. "Do you like my birthday dress? My aunt got it for me. Look what it does." She spun around and the dress billowed out, causing Nina to laugh.

"That's awesome. I love it."

"I wasn't sure you'd come."

The sound of Bret's deep voice reverberated along her nerves and sent heat rising in her neck. Adrenaline raced through her body. Every part of her was keenly aware of Bret's presence. His masculine scent swirled around her, and she could feel the heat of his body. She couldn't risk looking at him. She swallowed hard and found her voice. "I wasn't going to, but I promised Georgie. I'm here for her. No other reason."

"I understand."

The odd tone of his voice forced her to look at him. He was the image of dejection. His green eyes were dark and shadowed, his shoulders lowered. There was a hard line to his jaw she'd never seen before. Her heart went out to him. It wasn't easy for him either. Her attraction warred with her anger. Anger won out. She looked away. How could she still have feelings for this man?

She noticed Olivia, who was coming toward her, a sweet smile on her face.

"I hoped you would come. I'm glad you did."

Nina slipped her arm around the slender shoulders. "I am, too. I wouldn't miss it for the world. Have you been helping with the decorations? They are lovely."

"I did the playhouse and the cake table."

Bret took a step closer. "Nina, I want to talk to you."

"Not now. I want to enjoy the party." She walked off, holding Livvy's hand, but couldn't resist a glance back. Bret's shoulders slumped, and his hands were shoved into his pockets. He looked wounded. She shook off a flicker of sympathy. What else had he expected?

For the next two hours, the Sinclair house was full of noise and fifteen little girls all running willy-nilly around the yard. Finally Walt announced it was cake and ice-cream time. Nina helped serve and cleaned up more than one spilled dessert. Thankfully things were too hectic for her to do more than glance at Bret. But each time she did, her heart skipped a beat. There was so much to admire about him, his loving care of his girls, his respect for his father. His joy in watching his little girls be happy.

But he'd failed in one very important way. He'd failed her and her husband. How could she ever forget that or forgive him? She knew forgiveness was the answer, but it wasn't that simple. She couldn't just turn off the knowledge of what happened. His gross misconduct cost a man his life. Yet it didn't feel right somehow to put that label on him. It was as if he were two men, the kind, loving father and the cold, indifferent soldier. She could find no way to reconcile the two. Ever.

Georgie was bouncing on tiptoes when it was time to open presents. She thanked everyone for their gifts and ran and gave Nina a big hug after opening the book she'd given her about a ladybug and her children. The princess dress drew oohs and aahs, but when Bret brought out the last gift, a colorfully decorated box with a huge bow, Georgie's eyes grew wide. Bret set the box on the table and stepped back. Georgie fumbled a moment on how to open it, and then she lifted the lid, and the little dog with the spots peeked over the edge. The look of joy and happiness on Georgie's face brought Nina to tears.

"Oh, Daddy, thank you. He's just like I wanted." She hugged the wiggling pup close as all her friends gathered around, vying for a chance to hold him. Bret stepped in after a few moments and explained that it was time for the dog to rest. Soon after, the parents started arriving to pick up their daughters and the house quieted down.

Walt came outside with one more gift. Georgie tore it open to find a special dog bed and other items for taking care of her new friend.

Bret came to her side and held out his cell phone, showing her a picture of Georgie when she saw the puppy. It captured her happiness perfectly.

She smiled up at him. "This will probably be one of her best birthdays ever."

"I hope so. She really doesn't ask for much. I'll send you the photo if you'd like."

"Thank you."

"How's your little mutt?"

"Fine. She lets me know when people walk by and when a leaf falls off the tree."

Bret frowned. "A yapper, huh? Sorry about that."

She swallowed. The tension between them was intense. They were making meaningless chitchat to cover the awkwardness. She wanted to hug him and scream at him at the same time. Her heart wanted his comfort, but how could he possibly comfort her now?

Someone called to Bret that the puppy was stuck under the deck steps. Her chance to escape.

"Nina."

"I need to go. It was a nice party." When he moved off, she slipped into the front room and called a cab. It had been an emotional roller-coaster day, but she was so glad she'd come. Seeing Georgie so happy, surrounded by her friends, and sharing this day with the Sinclairs, had been wonderful. But ignoring Bret had been impossible, and her anger and hurt would flare up without warning.

Then there were the bittersweet moments when she remembered one of Molly's birthday parties. She missed the feeling of family, of sharing her daughter's happiness with her father. A father whom Georgie's father had allowed to die.

She walked from the room toward the front porch, but Bret blocked her exit. She considered pushing past him, but making physical contact with him always did unusual things to her senses, and she didn't want to risk that.

"What do you want, Bret? My cab will be here soon."

"Let me take you home. We need to talk. There are things I need to tell you."

"No, there aren't. There's nothing more to say."

"There are things Norm would want you to know."

Now he was being cruel and manipulative by putting the conversation on Chip and his role.

"Don't you want to know what he did? How he risked his life for a friend?"

It sounded like Chip. Always there for everyone. And for her and Molly, too.

"Please, Nina, I have to tell you."

She steeled her emotions and crossed her arms over her chest. "Fine, but it won't change anything."

Bret inhaled a slow breath as if caught off guard by her change in attitude. He led her into the front room and closed the French doors for privacy. He paced a few steps and then faced her.

"We were traveling to the next post, nowhere near the fighting. There was a convoy of four trucks. Norm and I were in the last one, and a close friend of his, a soldier he'd befriended, was in the vehicle ahead. It should have been a simple assignment. The camp had requested the services of a chaplain. Theirs had rotated home, and the replacement wasn't due for two weeks. It was a twenty-mile drive to the next location. But out of nowhere, we started taking fire. The truck in front of us hit an IED and flipped. Norm's friend was thrown out. Before I knew it, Norm bolted from the truck. I shouted at him to wait for me, but he ran ahead to his friend. Suddenly we started taking fire from the hills. When I reached him, he and his friend were both gone. Norm was half-shielding his body and clasping his hand. We lost five men that day. We shouldn't have lost any. Our intel was faulty. It was no one's fault. Just daily life in a conflict zone."

Nina sorted through the story Bret had told her, knowing in her heart that Chip would have done exactly as he described. If he thought someone needed him, he would run toward that person. Except once. Then he had run away—from her.

"I wanted you to know how it happened. I thought it might help somehow."

"It doesn't."

"Nina, he loved you. He talked about you all the time. He regretted leaving the way he did."

"But he did."

"Don't turn away from this, Nina. If you do, you'll be doing the same as Chip and Sylvia did—running away instead of facing the problem and working it out. I know we both failed at things in our life, but Sylvia and Norm failed, too. He shouldn't have run away to the service, and my wife shouldn't have abandoned our marriage and children."

The pleading look in his eyes touched her sympathies. If what he told her was true, then the only one at fault in the situation was Chip himself. The cab pulled up and honked. Her escape had arrived. "I have to go."

"Nina, wait."

She hurried to the cab, ignoring the voice inside that said she was doing exactly as Bret had warned. She was running away. But he was wrong. She wasn't running away; she was removing herself from an impossible situation. Not every problem could be solved by confronting it. Sometimes the only answer was to turn and walk away.

Bret watched the cab pull away and pounded his fist against the door frame. His frustration and hurt were tearing him apart inside, and he couldn't see a solution anywhere. He completely understood how she felt, but since telling her about Norm, he'd come to see that his failed marriage wasn't all his fault. There was much he could have done differently, things he didn't pay attention to, but Sylvia's decision to walk out was her own. She did it without telling him of her unhappiness, or making an attempt to work things out. Nina couldn't yet see that both she and Norm had made poor choices and made assumptions about each other that were wrong.

He turned from the door and walked into the living room. What worried him most was how she would react going forward. Everything was on the table now, but would she come to terms with it and move on? Or would she crawl inside herself again and close off the world? She'd changed so much, and now he'd shoved her backward. The thought made him sick to his stomach. All he wanted was to see her happy, and he'd done just the opposite.

"Daddy."

Bret smiled as Olivia came to his side.

"Where's Miss Nina? I wanted to talk to her."

"She's gone, sweetheart. She had some things to do."

"When will she be back?"

That was the million-dollar question. "I don't know."

Disappointed, his daughter left with a frown on her face. How was he going to explain this situation to the girls? They adored Nina and talked about her all the time. They wouldn't understand why she stopped coming.

The ringtone on his phone intruded into his thoughts. He pulled it out, wondering why Alan would be calling today. He was out of town and had regretted not being able to come to Georgie's party.

"Alan? What's up?"

"Good news, buddy. I'm here with my dad,

and he said it looks like our application will be approved. We should get the official word on Monday."

The news should have filled him with exuberant joy, but he could only muster a flicker of delight. "That's good news."

"It's better than good. It's great. This'll set Phase II on a path to success we never dreamed of. Think of the veterans we can help now."

Alan said a hasty goodbye, and Bret slipped his phone back into his pocket. It was good news. The best, but his heart was too shredded to appreciate it.

"Nina left without saying goodbye? That's not like her."

Bret looked up as his father walked into the room.

"Oh. I can tell by your expression that things between you didn't go well."

"I told her everything, all the details about Norm's death, but it didn't make any difference. I'm afraid it's over."

Walt frowned and set his hands on his hips. "For a decorated soldier, you sure give up easy. The Sinclairs don't cave when things get tough. Give her a little time. Then talk to her again."

"No. It won't do any good."

"Then I'll talk to her."

"No. Stay out of this, Dad. I mean it."

"Fine. You take some time to lick your wounds. Then get yourself over to her place and work this thing out. I'm telling you, she's the one for you. Make it work, or I'll write you out of the will and leave my millions to the dog pound."

"You don't have millions."

"Beside the point. Fix this."

Fix it. His dad made it sound so simple. But how? He'd told Nina everything, all the details. The only thing he hadn't told her was how he felt about her. Should he? Or was this a lousy time to bare his soul? She probably wouldn't welcome romantic attention from the man responsible for her husband's death.

There was no way around this, and there was too much baggage between them. He had to let it go.

Nina sat in her director's chair, spine stiff, trying to ignore the turmoil inside. The widows had gathered again, and she forced herself to focus on the ladies in her office. They needed her. She needed them. But she wasn't sure yet what she needed. For the last three days, she'd tried to sort through the things she'd learned, but all she'd managed to do was grow more confused.

Knowing how her husband had died, learning that it was his choice to break away to save a friend, had put a new light on things. Chip was responsible for his own death. He'd made the decision to abandon his protection, just like he'd made the decision to walk away from her.

But what part of that situation did Bret own? Shouldn't he have done more to stop Chip somehow? The memory of how quickly Georgie had slipped away from her came to mind. Was there any way to stop someone who had made up their mind to act? She knew the answer, but it didn't give her any satisfaction. For the last few nights, her dreams had been filled with visions of Bret's green eyes shadowed with torment and pain. His guilt over failing to save Norm had scarred him deeply. She couldn't ignore that fact.

Where did that leave her? Maybe it was best to cut her losses and go home and put all this behind her. But Kathryn wasn't due back anytime soon. Who would take over? She couldn't just walk out on her friend. But it was clear now that she didn't really belong here in Hastings. There was no future here. Bret would never allow her into his life, and she could never get past his part in Chip's death. She couldn't remain and hope to ignore Bret and his girls. They'd become too important to her.

Laughter drew her from her somber thoughts. She was ignoring her widows. She scanned the room and saw they were all looking at the door. Nina looked over her shoulder and smiled. She stood and greeted the newcomer. "Annie, I'm so glad you decided to come. Ladies, this is Annelle Sheppard. She'll be joining our group."

Nina made the introductions, and then she settled back into her chair. "Annie just moved to Hastings."

The ladies greeted the new member and asked the usual questions. Nina allowed it to go on for a short time, and then she began the session.

Her attention wandered as the women conversed about their week and the progress they'd made, or failed to make. The thought of leaving Mississippi left a knot in her throat. She'd come to like Hastings. She'd miss Dottie and her widows. Most important, being here had helped her reconnect with her faith. She didn't want to leave Bret and his girls, but how could she get past what Bret had done?

"My husband was killed in a car crash. He was driving drunk. He killed an elderly couple."

The sound of Annie's voice yanked Nina back to the session. "I'm so sorry."

Paula patted Annie's knee. "That must have been hard."

"Being left a widow was hard enough, but I don't know how to let go of what he did."

The ladies all offered sound advice to the newcomer. The very things she should be pointing out. However, Annie's words pierced Nina deeply. They were in a similar position. Both she and Annie needed to sever the guilt and sense of responsibility from the past. She understood how difficult that was, but she couldn't tell them to keep hiding, to stay put and not move ahead. She couldn't advise them to hold on to the old junk because it was comfortable, familiar and easy. Which was what she was doing.

The revelation nagged at her the rest of the evening, forcing her to take a painfully honest assessment of her situation. Much of what Bret had told her rang true about her husband. The part she found hard to accept was the affectionate way Chip had thought about her overseas. Was Bret making that up to make her feel better? She had to know, and there was only one source she could turn to for answers. It was time to read the letters.

As soon as she got home that night, Nina

turned on the light in her bedroom and went to the dresser, where she kept a small envelope. Her heart fluttered as she thought about what she might find inside the envelope as she pulled it out from the bottom of a drawer. Letters. All the letters Chip had sent. Letters she'd never read. She'd never been able to throw them away because, in the end, they were part of her husband, and she'd loved him dearly. She'd often wondered why she bothered to hang on to them given her feelings toward her husband. Now she realized it was for this moment. The moment she was finally strong enough to understand.

Sadie sat at her feet, looking up with sympathetic eyes. She reached down and patted the little head. "I guess if I want to learn the truth, I'll have to face whatever these letters have to say, huh, girl?"

She sat on the bed with Sadie snuggled at her side. Her hands shook and grew clammy as she pulled the first letter from the stack. The pulse in her neck throbbed. It took three attempts before she could break the seal and slip the half dozen sheets of paper from the envelope.

Chip had emailed when he first left, but she'd deleted those emails. The letters came later, probably when he realized she wasn't going to respond. One question loomed above the others. She spoke to Sadie, knowing the little dog couldn't respond, but finding strength in voicing her questions.

"If Chip regretted leaving like Bret claimed, then why had he?"

Nina unfolded the thin paper and started to read. Chip talked about the men he was meeting, his training and the soldier who would be assigned to him. The next letter was from overseas. He spoke highly of his assistant and about another soldier he was close to. A new dad eager to get home to see his son. He spoke of feeling safe but that even so far behind the lines as he was, no one was safe.

The last letter he wrote was about Molly. In it, he asked her to keep Molly's memory alive and to not close her heart to their little girl.

*Grieve and move on, my love. The only way to get past a tough time is go through it, not around it. Please, my love, stop blaming yourself for Molly's death. It wasn't your fault. It was mine. I tried to tell you several times, but you never heard me. You were so distraught, I didn't know how to help you when I could barely help myself. I'm the one who showed Molly how to release the child lock on the car door. She'd begged me over and over. She felt she was old enough to open her own door. I know she asked you several times, but you wouldn't listen.*

*It killed me to see you in such pain. Every day you withdrew deeper inside yourself, not talking or eating. You stopped driving and closed your practice. I didn't know how to reach you, and I eventually gave up. Leaving seemed like the only option. Time apart might give us both the space to deal with the loss.*

*But I regretted it the moment I left the country. I've hated myself for leaving you alone. It was a weak, cowardly thing to do. My only defense is that I was drowning in grief. A man of God should know to turn to the Almighty at those times, but God was the last one I wanted to hear from then. But I've found Him again. Here with these brave young men. I'm going to spend my time comforting the soldiers, and hopefully the Lord will comfort me in return.*

It wasn't her fault.

She scooped Sadie into her lap, struggling to understand this new information. She hadn't forgotten to lock the door. Chip approached her several times about the lock, but Nina had stood firm. In her eyes, Molly was still a baby.

"I should have paid more attention, been more sympathetic to Molly's request." Sadie whined and laid her chin on Nina's leg.

Neither she nor Chip had forgotten the lock. Molly probably undid it when she got into the car that day. So who was to blame? All of them or none of them?

"Someone has to take responsibility. Don't they?" Sadie had no words of comfort for her.

Her fingers grazed over the thin stack of letters. They'd answered many of her questions, but left her with a lot of soul-searching to do. And one big problem to sort out: Bret and his place in this new scenario.

The truth tried to surface, but she ignored it. She wasn't ready to examine her real feelings for Bret. It felt too much like being unfaithful to her husband and his memory.

## Chapter Twelve

Nina awoke the next morning with scratchy eyes and a headache from a restless night's sleep. Reading Chip's letters had upended all her assumptions, and she didn't know how to begin to unravel them. Was it possible she had it all wrong the whole time? She'd assumed Chip's long spells of silence were from anger, and his attempts to talk were because he wanted to remind her of her failure. But he was only trying to explain what had happened, and she'd refused to listen because she was convinced that she was at fault. Sadly, she'd been unable to see that Chip was suffering as much as she was.

The day Chip told her he was leaving, she'd erected another barrier around her heart, and when he'd died, she'd locked her emotions away, unable to process any more grief.

Her gaze lifted from the letters and scanned her apartment. She might not be directly responsible for Molly's death, but she was responsible for failing to understand her husband's grief. She'd been on a one-way path, and now suddenly it had branched into a different direction. What did she do now? Where did she go?

The coziness of her apartment became small and cramped, and the walls began to close in around her. She shivered. She had to get out of here, clear her head and think of something else. She had no appointments today, but at least at the office she could bury herself in work. It was late afternoon. She could walk to the office, get in a few hours' work and get back home before dark. Maybe the work and the exercise would tire her out and she'd be able to sleep tonight.

The walk to the office eased her anxiety, and studying patient files and handling a few business tasks had eaten up several hours. She glanced out her window and realized it was getting dark. She'd better be heading home.

Her cell phone rang. She blinked at the name appearing on the screen. Bret. Why would he be calling? They'd barely spoken all week. If he was calling to talk more, she wasn't interested. She had enough to work through as it was. Still, she didn't want to ignore him. She gritted her teeth and took the call. "Hello."

"Miss Nina?"

She strained to hear the faint voice. It sounded like a child. "Georgie? Honey, what's wrong? Are you okay?"

"Our car wrecked, and Daddy is asleep, and Livvy is, too. I'm scared."

*Oh, dear Lord.* Her heart pounded. "Are you hurt?"

"No."

"Do you know where you are?"

"We were going to Addie's house. She's having a sleepover."

Addie. Deb's little girl. That meant they must be on the main road. She tried to recall the name of the route. Twenty-Four? Twenty-Eight? But how could she find them? She had to call 911, but she had no idea where along that long highway they might be. She ran her hand through her hair, every nerve in her body screaming. She was helpless. "Georgie, you stay on the phone, okay? Don't hang up. But if you do, I'll call you right back, okay? How did you know to call me?"

"The pictures. Daddy showed me how to call Grampy by finding his picture on his phone, but he's not home, so I poked your picture. I want to go home. I'm scared."

"It's all right, Georgie. I'll be there as soon as I can. I'm going to call for help, so don't hang up." Nina grabbed the landline on Dottie's desk and dialed 911.

But she couldn't sit here and wait for them to find Bret and the girls. She'd go nuts. Adrenaline surged through her body, only to be followed by a tsunami of anxiety. Her gaze fell to the desk drawer. Keys. She had keys to Kathryn's car for emergencies. This qualified. But she couldn't. Getting behind the wheel of a car again was impossible.

"Miss Nina. Are you coming? I want you to come now."

Georgie's little voice pierced her fear. "I'm coming, Georgie." She grabbed up the keys and her purse, and she hurried to the back of the building. She strapped herself in behind the wheel of her friend's compact car, and her hands shook violently as she tried to insert the key into the ignition. Raw fear clawed up her throat and pulled her head down toward her chest. Her mind replayed the moment when Molly left the car, the squeal of tires, the impact.

But this wasn't then. Little Georgie needed her. Livvy and Bret could be seriously injured.

*Please, Lord, give me strength and courage. Take control of the car. Guide me to the people I love.*

In that instant, she realized that she did love them as if they were her own. Sweet, spunky Georgie, gentle-hearted Olivia, and Bret, the man she loved. Despite the truth about who Bret was and what he'd done, she could no longer ignore her heart. If anything happened to him… If she lost him… Tears stung her eyes.

She didn't have time for this. She had to get to her girls. She started the car and backed out. Her driving skills were rusty, and she hit the brakes too hard at first, but she quickly got the hang of it. She searched her memory for the way to Deb's farm. They'd taken the main road out of Hastings and driven until the landscape had become farmland and piney woods. But how far was that? Would she remember the farm when she saw it?

She scanned the darkness ahead for a car or blinking lights, taking care to check around every curve, all the while keeping up a conversation with Georgie on speakerphone, letting her know where she was and that she'd be there soon. But what if they'd ended up off the road and hidden?

The road narrowed, and the darkness thickened. How would she ever find them? Up ahead, an old iron bridge loomed. She remembered it. They'd crossed it shortly before arriving at Deb's.

"Georgie, did you drive over the old bridge before you crashed?"

"Uh-huh."

That meant she was getting close. A flash caught her eye. Off to the left, she saw a small red light. She slowed down and pulled over. Bret's SUV. It was angled deep into a ditch, the driver side down. "Georgie, I'm here, honey."

"I can't see you."

"You will." She climbed out of the car and slowly made her way over the uneven ground. Georgie's face appeared at the passenger side window. Nina tugged at the door. "Can you unlock the door, sweetie? Pull up that little knob." Georgie tried, but her fingers weren't strong enough. She started to cry. "Try the window. Can you push the button to make it go down?" Nina prayed that faint dashboard lights meant that the power windows would still work. She exhaled a breath as the window slid downward. Georgie leaned out, reaching for her. She probably shouldn't move the little girl, but right now, comfort outweighed protocol.

Nina wrapped her arms tightly around the little girl. "It's okay, sweetie. I'm here. The rescue people are coming to help Livvy and your daddy." Nina peeked in the back window. Olivia was slumped in her seat. She offered up a prayer. Bret was hunched over the steering wheel. It was too dark to see how injured he was.

By the time she climbed up the slope to the car, flashing lights appeared around a bend in the road. The emergency squad had arrived. The paramedics quickly went into action. One came to her, guided her to the back of the emergency vehicle and quickly examined Georgie. Thanks to the child safety seat, she was perfectly all right. Nina scooped her up and held her close as another medic examined Olivia, who was awake now and able to walk. Nina squeezed her little hand as she was handed over to the technician inside. A quick examination showed no serious injuries, but since she'd been unconscious awhile, they would take her to the hospital.

A police officer arrived and asked Nina questions about the accident. There wasn't much she could tell them, but Georgie proved to be helpful.

"A big animal ran in front of our car. Daddy almost hit it. Then we crashed."

The officer nodded and scribbled in his notepad. "Probably a deer. It's not uncommon out this way." He looked at Nina. "Are you her mother?"

"No. Just a family friend." No. She was more than that. Much more.

"Is there any other family we should notify?"

Walt. She'd forgotten all about him. "The grandfather, but Georgie said she couldn't reach him." Georgie still clutched her daddy's phone like a lifeline. Nina couldn't blame her. "Sweetheart, let me use the phone to call your grampy again, okay?" But the call went to voice mail, and all she could do was leave an urgent message.

Although she had been reassured that the girls were all right, it did nothing to alleviate the hot, twisted knot in her chest for Bret. How badly was he injured? Why wouldn't he wake up? The EMTs and the firemen who had shown up were still working to get him out of the car. It must be far worse than she could see through the window.

Finally the men appeared from the shadows, carrying a stretcher with Bret strapped in place. They slid it into the ambulance, but Nina couldn't see anything because she'd moved herself and Georgie away from the vehicle. Her heart raced. "Is he okay?" No one answered. She took the arm of the next medic to pass by, but he couldn't tell her anything. She wanted to scream, but with Georgie still in her arms, that was impossible.

A medic emerged from the back of the vehicle and came toward her. "We need to take the little one to the hospital to be checked out." He started to pull Georgie from her arms, but she began to cry and held on more tightly. She let go only after Nina promised to go to the hospital.

"Can I ride with you?"

The young medic shook his head. "No, ma'am. I'm sorry. We're taking them to County General Hospital in Hastings. You can catch up with them there."

Nina watched as the ambulance drove away, followed by the fire truck, and then the flashing lights of the police cruiser disappeared into the darkness. She started to shake. The adrenaline rush was wearing off, and she was crashing emotionally. The darkness wrapped around her, reminding her how far from home she was, how far from those she loved.

Quickly, she made her way back to the car and slid behind the wheel. It felt strange to be sitting in the driver's seat. She'd vowed to never drive again, yet somehow she'd managed to get all the way out here because Georgie had needed her. Now she had to make her way back and find the hospital. She had no idea where it was. Yet she was aware of a new sense of strength and confidence she hadn't known in a long time. More than that, she was aware of a swell of gratitude and thankfulness that she'd been able to drive again.

She offered up a heartfelt prayer of thanks. The Lord had taken over and given her the ability to reach the ones she loved.

The emergency room was crowded with people when Nina arrived. She'd made three wrong turns on the way to the hospital. She hadn't realized how little attention she paid to directions and landmarks when she wasn't driving.

She made her way to the main desk. "Can you tell me how Bret Sinclair is? He was in a car accident. They brought him and his two little girls here."

The nurse looked up. "Are you family?"

"No. A friend, but I'm the one that found them."

"Sorry." She handed a clipboard to an orderly and gave instructions to the person who approached the counter.

"But they don't have anyone else here right now."

"You'll have to wait in the main waiting area."

"Please, I just want to know if Mr. Sinclair is all right. He was unconscious when they brought him in."

"Sorry." The nurse turned away, leaving Nina fighting the urge to shout her demands from the top of her lungs just to get some information.

"Nina?"

Nina spun around and saw Jen Graves, one of her widows, coming toward her, dressed in a nurse's uniform. Nina suddenly remembered that Jen once mentioned she was a nurse. The sight of her friendly face raised her hopes.

"What are you doing here?" Jen touched her arm gently.

"Bret and the girls were in an accident. The girls are okay, but Bret was unconscious, and I can't find out how he is or where the girls are. I've tried to get hold of their grandfather, but he's not answering his phone. I'm so worried about Olivia and Georgie. They're all alone. They must be so scared. No one will let me see any of them, and they won't tell me anything at all."

Jen slipped her arm around her shoulders

and steered her away from the reception desk. "It's okay. I'll take care of it. Come with me. I'll let you sit in the family waiting area. Then I'll go see what I can find about the Sinclairs."

Nina took a seat facing the door so she could see Jen when she returned. At least now she would know how Bret was. She closed her eyes, praying for his recovery and asking for the girls to be safe and not afraid.

"Nina."

She opened her eyes to find Walt in front of her, his features drawn and tense. "I'm so glad you're here. I tried to call, but…"

"I know. I had my phone off. Stupid. I wasn't thinking. A nurse told me you were in here. She said they won't tell you anything?"

Tears formed in her eyes. "I'm not family."

Walt patted her shoulder. "Ridiculous. That's only a technicality."

Jen stepped to Walt's side. "I'll take you to see the children now, if you'll follow me. Then you can talk with the doctor, too, and he'll tell you about your son."

"I'll wait here."

Within a few moments, Walt returned, carrying Georgie in his arms and holding Olivia's hand. Nina hurried forward and embraced the girls. Georgie clung to her. "Are you okay?"

"They've released the girls, but I still don't

know much about Bret. This place is a zoo. No one knows anything."

"Mr. Sinclair. I'll take you to see your son now." Jen motioned for him to follow her.

Nina settled the girls beside her on the seat. "We'll be right here."

"I'll be back soon."

He and Jen disappeared, and Nina wrapped an arm around each little girl.

"Where's my daddy?"

"I don't know, sweetheart, but that's where Grampy has gone."

Livvy leaned her head against Nina's shoulder. "I want to go home."

"I know. We will as soon as we know how your daddy is."

It seemed like an eternity before Walt returned, and the somber look on his face plunged her heart into her stomach. "Walt?"

He gestured for her to calm down as he took a seat. "He's okay. Lots of bruises, but nothing broken. He has a concussion, and he's still unconscious. They're hoping he'll come around during the night."

"And if he doesn't?"

"They'll run some tests and see what's going on. But I know he'll wake up, so don't worry."

"Can we see him?"

"Not now. In the morning." He stood. "Let's get these girls home and settled." He patted her back. "You, too. You look like you could use some good strong tea. And maybe a hug."

Nina allowed him to pull her into a firm embrace. It was nice to have someone to lean on. "Come on, ladies. Let's go home."

Home. Nina knew in that moment that Bret's home was exactly where she wanted to be. She refused to think about all the obstacles still looming between them.

# Chapter Thirteen

Nina took another sip of her lukewarm coffee the next morning, her gaze focused on Bret's backyard, though not really seeing. It had been a long night. Fortunately, the girls went right to bed, but she hadn't been able to relax. If only she'd been able to see Bret, to make sure for herself that he was all right, she could have at least taken a measure of comfort from that. Instead she'd been left to worry and pray and try not to let her mind conjure up worst-case scenarios.

"You were up early."

She glanced over her shoulder as Walt joined her at the window. "How did you know?"

"I heard you."

"Sorry. I was trying to be quiet."

"You were. I didn't sleep much. However, I

suspect my granddaughters will sleep late this morning. They were worn-out. So I thought it might be a good idea for you to go to the hospital first this morning so you can see Bret. I think he'd like to see you when he wakes up."

"I don't think I'll be allowed."

"I've got that all arranged. Don't worry."

Nina didn't wait for a second invitation. A half hour later, she was walking into Bret's room. She'd hoped he would be awake, but his eyes were still closed, and his normally tanned skin was pale and drawn. The large white bandage on his forehead and the long scratch down his jaw made him look vulnerable. Tears stung her eyes, and she reached out to him, laying her hand on his arm, taking comfort from the warmth of his skin. The steady throb of his pulse under her fingertips eased much of her concern.

She couldn't stand to see the virile, athletic man she loved lying so helpless in the bed. *Please, Lord, let him wake up.* There was so much she had to tell him, and so much she'd come to understand. Like a kaleidoscope coming into focus, all the pieces of her life had finally coalesced last night. She'd recognized that she had plunged into denial after Molly's death and had become emotionally detached from life. Like a movie in slow motion, she'd seen how she and Chip had unintentionally confused and complicated an already difficult situation, causing each other to struggle alone with the loss and the grief. She didn't want that same lack of communication destroying what she felt for Bret and the relationship they had.

Her gaze went to the lashes lying against his cheeks and the straight nose and the full lips that had kissed her so tenderly. She leaned over him and stroked his hair off his forehead, her heart swelling with love for this man who had broken her barriers with his kindness and compassion.

"Please wake up. I have so much to tell you." Could he hear her? Jen had encouraged her to talk to him, assuring her that he could hear and respond, even if he couldn't speak.

"Bret, I need you to know I don't blame you for Chip's death. I've done a lot of thinking over the last few days, and I've realized that things happen that I can't control, but I can control how I respond. I realize that no one was to blame for Molly's death and both Chip and I reacted to the loss by closing ourselves off to one another. If we'd been truthful and open from the start, things might have turned out differently."

She slipped her hand in his and held it

tightly. "I don't want any more obstacles between us. I've thought about Chip, and going off without warning was normal for him. Like reactivating his service. And like Georgie taking off and not telling anyone." Now she was babbling. "Bret, I've come to care for you. A lot. More than a lot. You're important to me." She touched his cheek. "Bret, I love you."

Her gaze rested on his face, her heart hopeful that he would wake up and look at her with his beautiful green eyes and lashes fluttering.

A nurse walked in, and Nina pulled back from the bed, her cheeks warming. What was she doing? Baring her soul to an unconscious man in the middle of a hospital. Quickly, she left the room. Her admission of love would have to wait for another time. If ever.

The soft, sweet voice summoned him from the shadows. He recognized it instantly. Nina. And she was holding his hand, and her words seeped deep into his heart.

"I love you, too."

He opened his eyes, searching for the face he adored.

"I love you, too, son."

Bret squinted and forced his vision to clear. His dad was leaning over the bed. "Where's Nina?"

"She left. Said something about going to the office. You need to talk to her? Tell her what you just told me?"

"Not now." Besides, he'd probably imagined her saying those words. He'd awakened from his coma in the middle of the night, but he'd been in and out of sleep since then.

The girls huddled at the side of his bed.

Olivia patted his arm. "Are you awake now, Daddy?"

"I am." The sight of them was better than any medication the doctors could administer. Just having them here made him feel better.

"When can you come home?"

"Soon, I hope. Are you two okay?"

Olivia rested her head on his chest. "I love you, Daddy."

Bret stroked her hair with his hand. "Me, too, sweetheart."

Georgie held out her hands. "I can't reach you." Walt lifted her onto the side of the bed, and she wrapped her arms around her dad's neck. "I love you, Daddy."

Walt let out a grunt. "Sure is a lot of loving going around in here. The doctor told me you can go home today. Guess that means you have a harder head than I realized."

Walt lifted Georgie off the bed, and then he gestured to the girls to sit down. "I need to talk to your dad a minute. You want to tell me why you decided to put your car in a ditch?"

"There was a deer."

"That's what Georgie said, too. If it wasn't for her, you might not have fared so well. She's a hero."

Bret looked at his youngest. "What did you do, sweetheart?"

"I called Miss Nina, and she came and found us."

Bret looked at his father for an explanation.

"Georgie called her, and she hopped in a car and came to your rescue."

Bret studied his father's face. Was he kidding? "She drove?"

"She took Kitty's car to look for you." Walt raised his eyebrows and smiled. "When a woman makes up her mind about something, nothing will get in her way. I told you she was one tough lady."

Bret sorted through what his father had told him. There was only one thing that could push Nina to overcome her fear of driving. Love. Maybe he hadn't dreamed her words after all.

Nina stole a glance at her passenger. Walt had maneuvered things so she would drive Bret home from the hospital today. She suspected he was up to his usual matchmaking tricks, and she wasn't sure whether to punch the old goat or kiss him. Mostly she was grateful that Bret was all right. The thought of losing him had torn through her like hot barbed wire.

She glanced at Bret again. He appeared calm and relaxed, not at all like a man who'd been in an accident. She exhaled a small breath. Being near him was awkward, driving him made her anxious, but mostly, she was an emotional stewpot of tangled nerves. Had he heard what she'd said to him at the hospital? To her chagrin, she'd learned that he wasn't in a coma when she'd spoken to him, but merely asleep.

Bret smiled over at her. "I have to admit, seeing you behind the wheel of a car is weird. I'm used to you being over here."

"It's weird for me, too. I'm still uneasy about this driving thing."

"You're doing fine. It must have been terrifying getting behind the wheel again. Yet you managed to do it to save us. Why?"

"Because I care about you—all of you. Little Georgie was scared. I had to find her, and I had to get to you. I was afraid that you might be…" She clamped her mouth shut. No sense in making him feel uncomfortable.

Thankfully, she pulled up to the house, and

Bret climbed out. She accompanied him up the walk and onto the porch, but he didn't open the door. Instead he perched on the wide wall along the porch, held out his hand and drew her close, his green gaze capturing hers. "I'll never be able to repay you for what you did."

"No need." She attempted to pull her hand from his, but he held on.

"Thank you. You saved my family." He placed a kiss on the back of her hand. She looked into his eyes and saw the soft light of affection she'd seen many times before.

"Why did you leave? You didn't wait for my response?"

"What do you mean?"

"You said you loved me. I heard it. But when I opened my eyes, it was my dad looking at me, not you. Very disappointing."

Nina lowered her gaze. Her cheeks warmed with humiliation. "I wasn't sure you could hear me."

"I heard it all. Every wonderful word. But you were gone when I said I loved you, too."

She looked up, searching his face for confirmation of his words. "You do?"

He smiled and brushed a stray strand of hair from her cheek. "I think I started falling that first day, when I saw you on the sidewalk,

looking lost and confused and so out of place."
He tugged her a little closer. "You've opened
my heart again, Nina, to so many things. Like
you, I'd shut down my emotions for fear of
being hurt again and letting people down. But
I know now that I couldn't have stopped Sylvia from leaving or Chip from running to help
a friend."

He touched her cheek with his fingertips.
"My dad and my friends have been telling me
for a long time to let go of my guilt over Norm
and Sylvia. I finally realized that I wasn't getting anywhere doing it my way, so I gave it to
the Lord and trusted He'd work it out for the
best. And He did. Now I want to look forward
to a new future. One that will include you, if
you'll have me."

"Are you asking me to marry you?"

He glanced over his shoulder. "I don't see
anyone else here." He pulled her closer. "Will
you take me and my crazy dad, and my little
girls, and the dogs, and make me the happiest
man in the world?"

She slipped her arms around his neck and
kissed him. "Yes. I'd love to be your wife and
raise those precious girls. And the dogs, too."

"You think you can get used to Mississippi?"

"Actually, Kitty called the other day to tell

me they were staying in Spain for another six months and asked me if I would be interested in being her partner."

"Perfect." He kissed her firmly, a kiss full of promise for the future. "You know we'll never hear the end of this from my dad. He had you picked out for me from the get-go."

"He's a very wise man."

"Should we go inside and tell them?"

"So, you started falling in love with me that first day?"

He slipped his arm around her waist. "Someday I'll tell you how I've loved you for a very long time. Longer than you might guess."

# *Epilogue*

The sun glinted off the diamond ring on her finger, casting minuscule rainbows all over the room. Nina Sinclair couldn't keep the smile from her face. One short hour ago, she'd become Bret's wife. The small ceremony had been perfect for her new family. Walt had walked her down the aisle, declaring it was his right since he'd picked her out to start with. Alan stood up for Bret as best man, Dottie was her matron of honor and Georgie and Olivia were her flower girls. The little princesses were a vision in lavender dresses with ribbons down the back and puffy sleeves. They carried small nosegays of yellow flowers.

She'd chosen a tea-length antique white lace dress and a small hat and carried a small bouquet of white roses. Her fingers shook when she'd tried to put the ring on Bret's finger. He, on the other hand, had been calm and steady. The only sign that he was nervous came when he said "I do" and his voice trembled.

They'd decided to have a small wedding at Bret's church, with only family and close friends. Nina's mother had come, and they'd put the past behind them, confirming Nina's decision to come to Hastings as the best one of her life.

The reception unfolded in a blur of well-wishers and happiness. The only part that remained crystal clear in her mind was dancing with Bret. The world had disappeared, and she was only aware of being in her husband's embrace, moving with him around the floor, their gazes locked.

Now they had slipped away to a small room to change for the drive to New Orleans.

Bret stepped into the room, breathtakingly handsome in his tux, his green eyes capturing hers, his smile wide. Behind him two little girls hurried in and straight toward her. How she loved this family.

"Are you officially our mom now?" Olivia looked up at her.

"Yes. And as soon as we can, we'll make it legal, too." She hugged the child to her side. She and Bret had agreed that she should adopt the girls as soon as possible.

"Am I 'ficial, too?"

Bret scooped Georgie up, frilly dress and all, and gave her a kiss on the cheek. "Yes, Georgie, we're all official now. We are the Sinclair family."

"Spotty, too?"

"Yep, and Sadie."

Georgie grinned at Nina. "Can I call you Mommy now?"

The lump in her throat made it hard to respond. She nodded.

"You'll be the best mommy ever."

"I agree, princess." He set her down and gestured to Olivia. "Take your sister and go find Gramps. We need to change and get on the road, or we'll miss the boat."

Georgie hung back. "When can we go on our honeymoon?"

"After we get back." They had decided to take a short cruise out of New Orleans down to Cozumel for the two of them, and then, when they returned, they'd take a family "honeymoon" to Florida.

The girls hurried off, leaving Nina with a full heart.

Bret gave her a sweet, possessive kiss, and then he handed her a gift with a fancy bow. "I wanted to give you this before we leave."

She opened it and found a photograph of

the whole family taken at Bret's house the day they got engaged. She and Bret were in the middle, arms around each other. The girls stood in front of them, and Walt stood beside his son. Even the four dogs had been included. Everyone she loved was in this photo. Her vision blurred.

"Do you like it?"

"It's perfect." She wrapped her new husband in a loving embrace, sending up a grateful prayer. The Lord had restored her life and given her a family to love. This picture would go on the shelf beside Molly's and Chip's photos. Her family from the past and her family for the future. No one would ever take the place of Chip or Molly, but she could move forward now with new love and hope with Bret and her girls.

\* \* \* \* \*

Dear Reader,

Welcome to the first book in my new series. We'll be visiting a small city in Mississippi and three widows as they move forward and learn to love again.

This is a story I've wanted to write for a very long time, but it kept getting shoved into the background. When I finally started to work on it, I discovered it was going to be one of the most difficult stories I'd ever done. Dealing with Bret and Nina's grief and guilt was challenging, but as I worked through the story, the two characters became special to me.

Both Bret and Nina struggled with the inability to forgive themselves for past failures. In reality, neither one was to blame. When something bad happens, we want answers. We want to know why, and we want a reason so we can make sense of the terrible loss. But we must accept that God chose to give His creation free will, which can bring about painful events.

We are all guilty of harboring resentment and allowing grief to paralyze our recovery. Only by giving their grief and guilt to the Lord, completely, were Bret and Nina able to let go of their burden and find the courage to love and trust one another and step into their bright new future together.

I hope while reading this story you are able to find your way to forgiveness of yourself or someone else. It's what the Lord wants you to do.

All the best,

*Lorraine*

# HOME *on the* RANCH

**YES!** Please send me the **Home on the Ranch Collection** in Larger Print. This collection begins with 3 FREE books and 2 FREE gifts in the first shipment. Along with my 3 free books, I'll also get the next 4 books from the Home on the Ranch Collection, in LARGER PRINT, which I may either return and owe nothing, or keep for the low price of $5.24 U.S./ $5.89 CDN each plus $2.99 for shipping and handling per shipment*. If I decide to continue, about once a month for 8 months I will get 6 or 7 more books, but will only need to pay for 4. That means 2 or 3 books in every shipment will be FREE! If I decide to keep the entire collection, I'll have paid for only 32 books because 19 books are FREE! I understand that accepting the 3 free books and gifts places me under no obligation to buy anything. I can always return a shipment and cancel at any time. My free books and gifts are mine to keep no matter what I decide.

268 HCN 3760 468 HCN 3760

| Name | (PLEASE PRINT) | |
| --- | --- | --- |
| Address | | Apt. # |
| City | State/Prov. | Zip/Postal Code |

Signature (if under 18, a parent or guardian must sign)

## Mail to the **Reader Service**:
**IN U.S.A.:** P.O. Box 1867, Buffalo, NY. 14240-1867
**IN CANADA:** P.O. Box 609, Fort Erie, Ontario L2A 5X3

* Terms and prices subject to change without notice. Prices do not include applicable taxes. Sales tax applicable in NY. Canadian residents will be charged applicable taxes. This offer is limited to one order per household. All orders subject to approval. Credit or debit balances in a customer's account(s) may be offset by any other outstanding balance owed by or to the customer. Please allow 3 to 4 weeks for delivery. Offer available while quantities last. Offer not available to Quebec residents.

# READERSERVICE.COM

## Manage your account online!

- Review your order history
- Manage your payments
- Update your address

> ### We've designed the Reader Service website just for you.

## Enjoy all the features!

- Discover new series available to you, and read excerpts from any series.
- Respond to mailings and special monthly offers.
- Browse the Bonus Bucks catalog and online-only exculsives.
- Share your feedback.

*Visit us at:*

# ReaderService.com

RS16R